BECOMING GERSHONA

Nava Semel
BECOMING GERSHONA

TRANSLATED BY SEYMOUR SIMCKES

VIKING

VIKING
Published by the Penguin Group
Viking Penguin, a division of Penguin Books USA Inc.,
375 Hudson Street, New York, New York 10014, U.S.A.
Penguin Books Ltd, 27 Wrights Lane, London W8 5TZ, England
Penguin Books Australia Ltd, Ringwood, Victoria, Australia
Penguin Books Canada Ltd, 2801 John Street, Markham, Ontario, Canada L3R 1B4
Penguin Books (N.Z.) Ltd, 182–190 Wairau Road, Auckland 10, New Zealand

Penguin Books Ltd, Registered Offices: Harmondsworth, Middlesex, England

First published in 1988 in Israel as *Gershona Shona* by Am Oved Publishers
First American edition published in 1990
1 3 5 7 9 10 8 6 4 2
Copyright © Nava Semel, 1990
All rights reserved

This translation has been made possible in part through a grant from the
Wheatland Foundation, New York.
LIBRARY OF CONGRESS CATALOGING IN PUBLICATION DATA
Semel, Nava.   Becoming Gershona / Nava Semel.
p. cm.
Summary: Living in Tel-Aviv in 1958, twelve-year-old Gershona
experiences first love, learns a family secret, and crosses the line
between childhood and adulthood.
ISBN 0-670-83105-0
[1. Tel Aviv (Israel)—Fiction.] I. Title.
PZ7.S4657Be 1990 [Fic]—dc20 89-24845
Printed in the United States of America
Set in Sabon.

BECOMING GERSHONA

1

Out of the blue, they told me that Grandpa was coming the next day, and I never even knew I had a grandfather.

How could they have kept such a secret from me? I figured he must have vanished somehow—though I didn't say so. Apparently a person could disappear just as easily as your favorite toy and then show up when you least expected it, after you'd lost all hope.

He vanished years ago and my father went to America to bring him back. After six months, Daddy returned with a brand-new grandpa and a green used automobile named Plymouth. Nobody else on our street owned a car. Nobody had a gas stove, either. In our kitchen, of course, we had only a kerosene stove that smelled of smoke, so after each meal, we had to put it on the porch to air.

Not that I was the only girl around with a grandpa. Grandpas were common. But I alone possessed a father with a car. The kids in my neighborhood saw me differently now. They actually called me by my real name, instead of stretching it to Gershona-Shona, and for a week stopped calling me Gershona Primadonna!

When the two kids from the first floor knocked on our door, I overheard them ask my mother, "Is Gershona home? Has she finished her homework?" And Mom invited them in, raising her voice and her enthusiasm far too much. "Come in, come in!" And she hurriedly plopped a full bowl of taffy on the table. That amazed me, since at our home taffy was always reserved for special occasions.

Seated on my bed, I wouldn't touch those candies. No one spoke a word. They were too busy gorging themselves nonstop on the sticky squares. Hemda wiped her fingers on her skirt and waited for Avigdor to open his mouth, but only after he had gobbled up his last candy did Avigdor ask, "Can we see the new car? Up close, I mean. Maybe . . . maybe your dad'll show us the clocks inside. And maybe, on Saturday, if you ask him to, he'll agree to take me for a ride."

"Me, too!" said Hemda, her eyes turning rather vicious. "It was my idea to come up here!"

"Sure!" I said, but I really wasn't sure. Dad himself hadn't figured out how to cope with our new machine yet. That, I couldn't reveal. Alongside him on the front seat, he kept a thick manual of instructions in English, which he would read over and over, muttering to himself, "I don't get it. I just don't get it." I asked him why he bought the car if he didn't know how to handle one. Anyway, since he parked it so close to the curb, you couldn't see the full beauty of the four hubcaps, fresh from the factory.

2

"If your dad agrees to take us for a ride," said Avigdor, "you can join us in our garden." Those two let me help out only when they were desperate for someone.

As I jumped off my bed, the small bowl now containing just empty wrappers fell to the floor. Miraculously, it didn't crack. Mother heard the crash and immediately called out from the kitchen, "Anything break in there?" "No, no," I said and quickly accepted their request. I really wanted to work in their garden. "I'll get radish seeds," I said, already picturing the round violet-red dots hidden in the soil. Hemda and Avigdor exchanged glances, then Hemda made a face while saying, "We'll see; nothing's settled." Tilting his head, Avigdor examined the walls until his eyes stuck on the picture of a yellow sunflower right above my pillow. "Yuck," he exclaimed. "Is that supposed to be a flower? Who painted it?" I didn't reply.

"Flowers like that won't be in *our* garden," he asserted, shifting his attention to the closed drawers of my bureau. "Do you have a lot of toys?" Not waiting for an answer, he pulled a drawer open.

Hemda yanked his sleeve, urging him to leave. But since I wanted them to stay longer, I even took out the whole drawer as an inducement. Rarely did I have any kids visit me. Mother would ask, "How come they never want you to play with them?" And I'd shrug my shoulders and bite my tongue until it hurt. My teeth actually notched my tongue, like the saws the boys use at school, in shop.

Avigdor demanded, "So do you have any or don't you?"

And I quickly said, "I have a new grandfather, too. Want to see him?"

Hemda burst out laughing. "She has a grandfather? So

3

what! He's no toy—just a person! You didn't buy him. What's so special about your grandpa?"

I explained, "He's come from America. . . ."

But that, too, didn't impress them. They ran to the stairwell, with Avigdor shouting, "Don't forget . . . your dad's new car, you promised!"

I figured that maybe, even in America, a grandfather is just a grandfather. But I couldn't understand why I neglected to tell them that he *was* different, in a way. My grandfather was blind.

2

Mom and Granny made a trip to the port to meet them. Mom didn't know anybody who could take care of me in the meantime, but she asked our neighbor, Simha, if she would give me lunch and let me stay with her till evening. Very ceremoniously, she handed me the key, something she had never done before, and said: "Guard it well." As if it were made of gold. After all, it was just an ordinary metal key, and Mom didn't even know that you could enter the apartment by the back porch, if you wanted. But I never told her that I once did it, because she would have fainted.

I went over to Simha's. She was exactly the opposite of her name, which means joy. That happens sometimes. Sometimes a woman with the name Bella is an ugly witch, and a man called Shalom never stops arguing with everybody, and a dog named Hero runs away even from cats. I got bored, so I asked Simha for permission to go back to my apartment. First she was reluctant, but then she agreed. "I'll take a short nap," said Simha. "Have you finished your homework?"

It was the first time I had ever opened our front door with a key, and it wasn't so complicated. Many of the other kids in my class already had house keys, but not me. When I asked Mom why not, she answered, "Because I'll always be home."

I was really glad that they'd left for the port without me. I knew I would have a chance now to roam around the apartment on my own and explore all sorts of things. I knew that Simha wouldn't notice if I was gone for one minute or thirty. She didn't pay attention to details. Her Hebrew was full of grammar mistakes, which I never bothered to correct. Her mistakes were so funny.

Naturally, Mother had shut all the blinds, and to make the apartment even more secure, she had closed the curtains, too. Nevertheless, the light managed to sneak inside. The kitchen table was set with plates and cups, as if any minute the meal was about to be served. A covered pot stood on the kerosene stove. She had already sent me out for ice yesterday. And there was something else on the table, under the salt container that looked like a scale balance.

A photograph, which Mom had placed under the salt container so it wouldn't fly away, God forbid. But what was she afraid of? How could any breeze enter the apartment if all the windows were shut tight! And if a gust of wind ever managed to burst through somehow, the photograph wouldn't have been protected by that small salt stand because it toppled over so easily. Carefully, I pulled the photo free, without spilling a grain of salt. It was of a man in uniform standing bolt upright. His hair was well-combed—each strand in place, perfectly parted, as if he had prepared especially for this moment. The photograph was old. I could tell because of its brown, faded color and missing corners. I turned it over, and on the back were written some words using the Hebrew alphabet but sounding like another language. I tried reading it slowly. "Tei-yereh"—I recognized that as the Yiddish word for "dear." I knew Yiddish from Granny, but I didn't realize it was written in Hebrew script. Interesting how it ever came to share our letters. After all, Yiddish is a language for old people. The next word after this one was Regina—my granny's name.

I understood at once that the man in the photo was the grandfather who was arriving. Maybe he, too, kept a brown picture of Granny all these years. On the ship, he'd have time to remove it from his pocket and see how Granny looked as a young woman, when they first met. His chest—in the photograph—was decorated with all sorts of medals, exactly like the figures in last year's Purim costume parade. These had to be medals of honor, awarded by some king or prince for his bravery, which already made me proud of this strange grandparent of mine. I told myself: Maybe that explains his absence. Obviously he was working for somebody important.

On the boat, Dad must have deluged him with questions the whole voyage. Where was he all this time, and how did he really vanish? Mom told me that the trip from New York to Haifa took two weeks, and I'm sure that was enough time to answer every conceivable question. When

I thought of Daddy, a warmth rushed through me. I missed him so. Every week I got a letter from him, but six months is a long time, and I spoke with him on the telephone only once. Actually, we didn't have a telephone—only our neighbor Simha had such a marvelous invention. It was black and heavy, with two chrome buttons that always felt cold under my fingertips—I was afraid that the connection would get cut if I so much as brushed them by mistake.

As soon as Simha came to mind, I put back the photograph under the salt shaker, which I tried to place in exactly the same spot as before. But I already noticed that a few grains of salt had scattered onto the the tablecloth. I shoveled them under one of the plates so mother wouldn't notice. When I locked the door after myself, I was scared that the bolt might snap. Who knows how locks react to somebody like me who is a perfect stranger to them.

On tiptoe, I returned to Simha's apartment. She had left her door slightly ajar for me. I heard her snoring. I could breathe easy. She had no inkling of how long I'd been gone. I waited at least an hour for her to wake up. When she finally did, she said, "I didn't really sleep, I just took a catnap." I smiled to myself. Adults never like to admit that they sleep in the afternoon. As if they were afraid that someone would yell at them for wasting time. What difference does it make if they sleep? They don't have any homework to do!

Simha stretched and said, "It'll be interesting to see if your granny recognizes him." I didn't answer. I asked myself how she knew all about it, when *I* only found out yesterday that I had a grandfather in the first place. Simha had come to Israel from Bengasi in Libya. Her cabinet was always loaded with shiny copper utensils. For hours she would polish them. A dust rag always peeked from her apron pocket, in case she discovered a stain that had escaped her eagle eye.

Simha had no husband, just three grown-up sons whose pictures, along with the grandchildren, she displayed in a straight row above the cabinet. She called her husband "my deceased," and would always quote what he'd said when he was alive. Every Friday evening, her whole family would gather at her apartment. For five consecutive minutes, you could hear the pitter-patter of their footsteps on the staircase. In the past few months, they had added the wheels of a baby carriage that they dragged up the steps. One wheel squeaked—that's how we knew for sure they had arrived. Sometimes they would invite me to play with the baby, who gurgled in excitement and stretched out his hands to me.

On Passover Seder night, her daughters-in-law came upstairs almost in a procession, their hands laden with heavy pots and baking pans full of pastries. Around our Seder table sat three women—Mom, Granny, and me. We listened to the festive furor bursting from the apartment next door. Mother tried to comfort me, saying that Daddy was thinking of us at this very moment, but I had the impression that she was really just trying to convince herself. That's when I decided to include Elijah the Prophet as an active member of our Seder and told myself that, as far as I was concerned, he could fill in for Daddy.

Simha prepared a glass of tea for herself and for me,

using a whole mint leaf in each glass. She was worried. "Who knows," she said, "maybe the boat's late. My deceased used to say that if a ship were such a trustworthy invention, God Himself would have boarded Noah's ark." Her words were hardly encouraging. Already I imagined my father and grandpa swimming ashore, both holding on to one life preserver.

Suddenly Simha laughed to herself. When I asked her why, she answered, "I hope your father located the right grandparent. After thirty-five years, it would be easy to make a mistake and bring back a total stranger."

"Simha," I asked, "do you know what the word *primadonna* means?"

"Somebody who thinks well of herself," said Simha. "You know anybody like that?"

I looked into the mirror in the hallway and saw a skinny short girl with two brown braids. Swivelling my head, I strained to see if the part was in the middle.

Simha entered the mirror. "Your grandmother will be able to recognize him." She sounded sure of herself. "A woman never forgets her man."

3

Night came, and they weren't back yet. Simha went into the kitchen to prepare supper for me. I've noticed that whenever she gets nervous, she begins cooking. She even let me take out the copper utensils from the cabinet and set them on the table. She didn't know what to do with me. We played tic-tac-toe, the only game she was familiar with, and she lost three times in a row, until she gave up in disgust. I said that maybe the road from Haifa to Tel-Aviv had stretched like the rubber waistband on underwear, but she didn't find that funny. Finally, she let me wait for them at the window and didn't add the usual warning not to lean out. That was Mother's fixed rule, even though all our windows were barred.

I sat and scanned the street. Only from Simha's apartment could you see all of it, from end to end. I discovered that the bus came every half hour, and when it pulled out from the stop it gave a grunt of sorts, as if it were choking. I saw all the neighbors returning from work, toting briefcases and shopping bags. Mr. Rosen, Hemda and Avigdor's father, carried their usual loaf of bread under his arm. If he didn't bring home a loaf of bread each evening I could hear his wife scream at him.

Before darkness covered everything like a blanket, I saw a van stop in front of the last house at the end of the block. Two guys unloaded some chairs, a table, and trunks. I saw a boy emerge from the back of the van. Actually, his face wasn't visible, but I could tell that he was tall and that he moved his body very sparingly. Some man, apparently his father, held him by the shoulder. They didn't speak to each other, they just watched the workers unload more boxes and set them down on the sidewalk. The boy's father paid them, and then the workers began lugging the belongings into the house. Poor guys, I thought. Why wouldn't the other two men help them?

The father followed them, but the boy remained standing on the sidewalk. Suddenly he ran over to one of the trunks and started digging into it. He quickly unpacked all kinds of stuff, strewing it all over the sidewalk, until he found what he was looking for. The darkness had already put on several more layers, and the street lamp couldn't show me what it was that the boy was holding. Not giving up, I strained my eyes until I was scared he might somehow sense that I was spying on him. But I was still unable to make out that mysterious object.

Simha asked, "Want some cocoa, Gershona?" I didn't like the way she said my name. Then she suggested that I go back and get my pajamas. Our apartment was absolutely quiet. The photograph rested under the salt shaker, and I couldn't help myself, I had to take another look. Grandpa suddenly looked different this time.

I fell asleep by the window. The pane was warm where my forehead leaned against it. I woke when Daddy touched my shoulder and said in his softest voice, "I'm back home, Gershonita." Nobody else called me that.

I thought I was dreaming, till the moment I was awake in his arms. My eyes were still sticking together, but I could immediately distinguish a man standing by the wall. He wore a dark shirt and a tie. Although he didn't look anything like the man in the photograph, I knew that he was the grandfather that Daddy had brought back from America. His eyes were wide open, and how he glared at me! Chills went up my spine.

4

Hemda and Avigdor didn't forget my promise. Come Saturday, at nine on the dot, they knocked at my door. Behind them stood somebody else—their cousin Haggai, who was visiting from his kibbutz. I wanted to say that Haggai wasn't part of the deal, but I remembered the flower garden and my dream of radishes. I'd already managed to collect the seeds from the gardener and had placed them in a small paper bag under my pillow. I figured it was worthwhile to stimulate them before sticking them in the ground. Some seeds have it so good that they forget to sprout—like animals that hibernate all winter. To me, it's important that my garden should have wide-awake seeds. I struggled over whether it was right to leave them under my pillow. There they might just fall asleep because of me—my sleep could be contagious. But since I'm always running around in my dreams, they'd have no choice but to tag along.

I am positive that seeds grow by night and not by day. Daytime is something they acquire only after they emerge from the ground. Just like human seeds. An infant in the belly is called an embryo because it's embroiled in the body. Secretly I would peek at my mother's belly and wonder if she, too, contained an embryo inside her, like a radish seed that nobody had been able to awaken yet.

Daddy was the one I had to wake up. When I shook him a few times by the shoulder so he'd get up, he groaned, "But I like to sleep on Saturday."

"You gave your word!" I told him. And he went downstairs in slippers and pajamas. He was so muddled that he forgot the keys to the green Plymouth, and I had to go back up to get them. He inserted the key into the slot, turned it, but nothing happened. They sat quietly, waiting patiently. Daddy turned the key again. But it was as if the car didn't even have a motor. All we heard was a tiny click, and the impudent car wouldn't budge. Meanwhile, I kept repeating to myself, "Come on already, come on!" And I begged God to do something about it.

Daddy rubbed his eyes and said, "I'll try one more time. Tomorrow I'll take her to the mechanic."

"Her or him?" asked Avigdor.

Daddy shrugged his shoulders. "Take your pick."

"I prefer him." Avigdor puffed up his chest. "A car is for men."

Daddy promised to take Avigdor for a ride next Saturday, but I felt miserable. There was no point in bringing up the flower garden now. I asked them, "Would you like to come upstairs? We have more taffies and pretzels."

"Pretzels!" said Haggai, all excited. Apparently, in his

kibbutz the children got pretzels only on holidays. We climbed up the stairs. Mother hadn't come out of the bedroom yet, and I got the pretzels from the bench that had a lid that lifted. That was where we stored all sorts of edibles in case of an emergency, like a blockade, for instance. Deep inside that bench lay sacks of rice and sugar from the days of the Sinai Campaign, two years ago. Mother wouldn't allow us to remove them, saying that we couldn't know when we might need those items.

The three of them waited for me to open the bag, and then they quickly stuffed their faces and their pockets with as many pretzels as they could handle. We stood in the kitchen. The door was half-closed. Somebody's hand opened it. They turned their heads to see who was coming. I didn't have to turn my head, because I knew it was Grandpa's hand that was groping along the walls.

His footsteps made a dragging noise, as though somebody were being forced to haul something very heavy. That was how he found his way around the house. His hand probed the edge of the door, and his fingers tapped and danced like small snakes. Avigdor and Hemda were transfixed. Haggai jumped backward. I think all of them were terrified.

Grandpa entered the kitchen and asked in Yiddish, "Who's here?"

I walked over to him and said in Hebrew, somewhat angrily, "Gershona and friends." It was awkward saying my name in front of them; I especially didn't want Haggai to hear it. Tomorrow he'd be telling his whole kibbutz about a girl with an ugly name that he met in Tel Aviv.

"Who's that weird man?" asked Haggai. "Why does he hug the walls as he walks? Is he sick or something?"

"He scares me," said Hemda. "Let's get out of here! You liar. Some car! It's just a green tin can that he got in America."

They stormed out, and I didn't even follow them. I sat scrunched on the bench with the liftable lid. Grandpa continued groping and feeling his way until he found a glass on the shelf. He carefully set it down on the marble sink counter. His other hand went strolling in the air in search of the spigot. Then it passed from the round cold-water tap to the round hot-water one. Very slowly he turned it, as his body backed away a bit so the water wouldn't splash him in a sudden burst. He placed the glass under the stream of water. It was hard for me to breathe. My whole body was tense. I wanted to see if he would pull his glass away in time. With his free hand, which was leaning against the sink, he closed the tap. But he didn't drink, he just set the glass cautiously on the marble, and then craned his body and said, "Somebody's here." He didn't ask, but stated a fact instead.

I slowly rose and stood still, on my toes. My goal was to slip out of the kitchen without his knowing it, but his hand reached out and caught me. His powerful fingers wouldn't let go of me, no matter how much I struggled against them.

"Your friends left," he said.

I began crying soundlessly. But my eyes gushed, and I dried my cheeks with the back of my hand and my sleeve.

"You're crying, no?"

"How do you know? You can't even see!"

Grandpa laughed. "To see you, I don't really need eyes."

We spoke in a mixed language. Half Yiddish, half Hebrew. Two tongues in one. He understood me, and I understood him.

"Sometimes it's better not to see at all!" I wanted to get him angry. He looked like a man who easily lost his temper. I remembered all those medals of honor in the photograph. Apparently he was on the verge of getting annoyed. Then he picked up the glass from the marble counter. Without groping in the least, he found it at once and stretched it toward me. Again without error, he angled it directly to where I was standing.

"It's important that you drink. Your eyes lost all their water, so you have to fill up the irrigation channels. Otherwise you won't be able to cry again."

I took the glass from his hand but didn't drink. Who needs tears, I thought. Who wants something that makes you ashamed of yourself?

The glass stood all day on the table in my room. Now Granny sleeps with me. Grandpa sleeps in the living room on the folding bed. I didn't ask why they weren't sleeping together. Maybe they needed time to get used to each other again.

The cloudy water in the glass grew transparent. I lay in bed and gazed at it. To me it looked like a small sea whose colors had faded. I pulled out the bag of seeds from under my pillow, and I scattered them inside one of the flower pots on the windowsill. I poured all the water in the glass on the seeds. Luckily they weren't tears. The salt would have destroyed them. There was one question that troubled me the whole time, but only after many days had gone by—when Grandpa and I had become friends—did I dare to ask him, "Tell me, can a blind person cry? Weren't his eyes taken away from him?"

5

They acted very strangely. I noticed that whenever Grandpa entered the room, Granny was quick to leave. And when she came out to the porch, he didn't even turn his head to her, though he knew she was standing there. Also, when she handed him a plate, she made sure that her hand didn't touch his. Suddenly the house became crowded and the whole arrangement of who slept where and with whom got on our nerves! My only refuge was the kitchen table, where I did my homework in the afternoon. Daddy and Mom left for work in the morning, and I went to school, so what Grandpa and Granny did together during those hours I had no idea.

Whenever I came home, I would find each of them in a separate corner and silent. Already I began thinking that maybe blindness impairs speech. I wanted to suggest that they bring up old memories. There had to be some subject they were both interested in. After all, once upon a time, even if it was a million years ago, they met and decided to marry, and even had a son. But I didn't dare. I had the feeling that she was angry at him for coming back.

Granny had lived with us from the time I was born. Maybe she was living with my parents even before that, when they first arrived in Israel. She was my only granny. On Mother's side, there wasn't anybody left. Granny was unlike all the other grannies of my classmates or those on the street. She spent most of her time embroidering tablecloths, and if I ever disturbed her, she would wave her silver thimble at me. Even before Grandpa showed up, she wasn't such a great talker. Once I asked Mother if people kept quiet only when they had nothing to say, and Mother answered that some people can talk and still keep quiet. Every evening, Granny waited by the window for Daddy to come home safely from work. Even though all he had was an office job. The worst thing that could have happened to him there was a thick book falling on his head.

She would stand next to the window, all tense, her lips moving. I don't think she was actually talking to herself. For example, I talk to myself only in front of a mirror. Maybe she thought the window was a mirror.

Now a competition was going on between Grandpa and Granny on the porch. Before he came outside, she would arrange a small chair for herself and a table for her sewing kit. As soon as he showed up, he quickly placed an armchair in the other corner. While Granny sat there, her head bobbed from side to side as if the wind were blowing it around—but our porch never caught a single breeze. Now and again she would blurt out a pair of words, *"Oy vay."*

That's a Yiddish groan. You don't groan like that when you're sad or in pain, only when you're sitting alone on a porch and sure that nobody can hear you. Because if you say *oy vay* to anybody, he'll immediately answer back with his own *oy vay*, and soon there'll be a whole pile of them.

Once I sneaked up behind her and whispered *"Oy vay."* At first she didn't know where that voice was coming from, but when she discovered that it was my little prank, she grabbed hold of me, and that evening she informed Mother that "the girl was impudent" and there was no proper education in this country. They were all "barbarians," she said, who "forgot European manners." I asked who the barbarians were, but Mother had no patience to answer me. After standing on her feet for hours in Starkman's Grocery, she was pretty nervous, and she said that Daddy would have to explain it. But she forgot that Daddy was in America then.

Also, Granny didn't let me touch her embroidered tablecloths; she would only let me watch how the needle galloped and the thread tightened into tiny stitches, like crumbs left on the tablecloth after a holiday meal. In her eyes, embroidery was the most important thing in the world, and she unwillingly assisted Mother with the housework. In particular, she refused to help mop the floors, and Mother complained that one day her back would break from all her floor washing. When Granny wasn't doing embroidery, she would spend her time reading German novels, and she'd walk to the library dressed in her best outfits as if she were on her way to a party. Her dresses had lace collars, stiff from too much starch. And their sleeves were trimmed with delicate, transparent linen. If only I could have a dress like that some day. In summer, she regretted that she couldn't wear her gorgeous dresses, and Mother would say to her, "Regina, you're just going to the library, why waste the dress? Save it for some happy occasion." Granny would clap her hands together and sigh. "Really now, what happy occasions will I have?"

And when at long last, the happy event arrived from America, she didn't celebrate. Until the moment they left for the port, she kept on embroidering vigorously, as if she wasn't the least bit excited over what was about to happen, and she simply said that now was the time for her to finish the tablecloth that had the roses on it. Mom urged her to hurry up, but she asked if she could drop by Simha's place for a moment to leave the tablecloth for her. As I waited for them there, I saw how Simha gazed at the tablecloth as though it were one of her own precious copper utensils.

Actually, Granny was Simha's only friend. In Granny's willing ear, she could pour whatever her deceased had once told her.

As for the reunion of Granny and Grandpa, I couldn't fathom what that would be like. How do people react who haven't seen each other for a million years? Is there a special embrace for such a meeting? As Granny's best friend, Simha knew much more about all this than I did—of that I was certain.

On the day Hemda and Avigdor started their flower bed, Granny and I had a fight. Right after school, they went outside armed with a rake and shovel. I saw how hard they were working, smoothing the earth and weeding the wild grass. Hemda looked up and caught me peeking at them from the window, but she paid no attention.

Granny grumbled, "They'll dirty the entranceway. Barbarians!" And she ran downstairs to rescue the laundry.

"Flowers don't just grow on tablecloths," I called out. I didn't mean to be rude.

"What do you know about flowers?" She was so wounded and I didn't understand why. Her voice was furious. "Once they incinerated live people, and beside the crematoria they planted flower gardens. It wasn't long ago."

Grandpa's hand touched her. That was the first time he spoke to her in my presence. "Let the girl go downstairs. If she gets a little dirty, so what?"

"Gardening is for professionals and not children. And not even for adults who don't know what it's all about."

"Regina," he said, "you don't have to be angry at the whole world."

She stood in front of me, and her eyes glinted. Grandpa took her hand and began patting it. She looked at him and made no attempt whatsoever to free her hand as she said to me, "Go over to Simha and bring back my rose tablecloth. I forgot it was there."

I had no desire to go, but I did. My curiosity mounted. I wanted to know what would happen next. Whether they would continue a conversation.

Simha wouldn't return the tablecloth right away. First she spread it out to check how many unembroidered roses were left. "Just three more roses," she said, "not bad at all. She'll finish it on time. She's a wonderful worker, your grandma. Maybe if she had mailed him a few tablecloths in America, he wouldn't have sent her any divorce papers by mail."

"By mail, what?" My voice suddenly trembled.

"Divorce papers," said Simha. "Don't you know that your grandfather and grandmother are divorced?"

All sorts of shrieks penetrated the house. Hemda and Avigdor, along with some other kids who had joined them, were howling with joy. I thought I was going to faint any minute. A divorce in our family? . . . and between Granny and Grandpa no less. Who ever heard of such a thing?

When I was back in our apartment, I felt as if my knees were shaking. I could have sworn I heard Granny whispering behind the door, "Sshh . . . not in front of the child," and only then she opened it. Apparently I had imagined the whisper because everything was back to the way it was before. Grandpa sat in his corner and Granny in hers, both of them silent. But on her cheeks flushed two red roses.

6

Every day on the way to school, I'd stop for a few minutes to check their garden. I was relieved to see that not a single stalk had grown in the meantime. All it had were several tiny mounds that looked like granules of shredded chocolate. Hemda hurried out of class to water the garden. She would grab her knapsack, quickly copy the homework off the blackboard, and exit running. She wouldn't even turn her chair upside down. I thought about my flowerpot in the window, and asked myself if it really was thirsty only twice a week. The rules for plants are completely different from the rules for people, the gardener explained to me. But have plants ever told anybody all their secrets?

My pot, too, hadn't sprouted even one small leaf. To be absolutely sure, I ran my fingers through the topsoil, in order to determine if something was there anyway, no matter how invisible. That's how I fingered my gums after

I lost a tooth. And I felt the new tooth long before you could see it.

Mom asked, "What did you plant in the pot? Is there a flower waiting to bloom?" Then she advised me to plant a geranium, which roots very fast, or a wandering Jew. What a strange name for a plant! It's hard for me to believe that tiny suitcases hang from its leaves. I didn't tell Mom that I planted radishes in the pot. She knew nothing about plants; she just felt that a child should eat all sorts of vegetables. At supper, she saw to it that I had a whole tomato on my plate, because a tomato contained a lot of vitamins. She always said the word "vitamins" as if it were some mysterious, magical substance and, if I ate enough of it, I'd be able to fly or grow to the ceiling. Meanwhile, her sharp eyes would investigate whether I had finished everything to the last vitamin.

I had my own tactics—stuff everything in the hollow of my cheek and say that I had to use the bathroom, where I spit it all out. Ten times a day, Mother would exclaim, "Don't forget that you mustn't drink after eating vegetables and fruits! And never eat a cucumber with the peel, it's dangerous. And wash it well—at least three minutes under the faucet."

And I planned on gorging myself on radishes right from the ground without washing them. I'd just clean them off with my fingers. By now I'd perfected my system of pot gardening. With an old popsicle stick, I would rake the soil, and with Granny's eyedropper, I'd water the seeds. The seeds must have thought it was raining. That small flowerpot became my most important activity, even more than collecting colored napkins.

Downstairs they continued to work in that flower garden of theirs, at first diligently, but after a while, their devotion slowly began to fade. Some days Hemda forgot to water it, and once I heard her scream at her brother and claim it was *his* turn!

"Bah! I hate your silly garden!" he roared back. "You planted the laziest flowers!"

"As lazy as you!" she said brazenly. "You always prepare for your tests at the last minute."

"Shut up! You water them too much. How can they grow if they're rotting in your puddles of water?"

"You idiot! I'll get Gershona Primadonna to help me. Have you seen the way she stares at our garden? She thinks we planted flowers made of gold."

I didn't listen anymore. I ran upstairs to the apartment. The hell with their garden! Let nothing grow there, not so much as a single shoot!

I pressed the doorbell, but nobody answered. I considered walking over to Starkman's Grocery and getting my mother. She worked there mornings when Starkman's wife had to go to the clinic for her swollen legs. She was an unfortunate woman. The Nazis had done all sorts of experiments on her, that's what I heard, and that was the reason they had no kids. Sometimes I would suddenly get frightened that my mom, too, had terrible things done to her, and maybe that explained why I had no brothers or sisters.

Mrs. Starkman burst out weeping in front of her customers, but she distributed candies to any children who frequented her store. She pinched the little ones on the cheek, saying, "Darling, just stay healthy." Starkman was very satisfied with my mom. He said she was the most diligent salesperson he had ever come across, and she even kept exact records of all credit transactions in his brown ledger, which was practically in shambles.

Just as I was about to leave, the door opened. "Gershona's home," said Grandpa and already started closing the door. I don't know how he suddenly sensed it was me, because I hadn't said a word; maybe it was my scent. He reached out exactly where I'd put my knapsack and dragged it inside.

"It's very heavy," said Grandpa. "What are you lugging there, stones? Is that what you're learning in the land of Israel, how to construct it as fast as possible? All day I hear them building. Do you know how tall the buildings are in New York? They even have a special name. Skyscrapers. I pity any cloud that passes by. It'll get cut in two." Grandpa laughed, and his eyes closed.

I was shy about looking at his eyes. I only peeked stealthily, so he wouldn't sense what I was doing. Precisely because he was blind, I imagined that he somehow saw by other means. Maybe through his skin.

Grandpa made sweeping outlines in the air. He drew one line over my head.

"Were you a builder, too?" I asked.

"I plucked chicken feathers for a living."

I was delighted. "Feathers to fill pillows?"

I remembered that Hemda and Avigdor once told me about a pillow fight they had at home, and how a pillow split open and the feathers flew into all the rooms. That

29

night, I even found a few feathers in our place. If I ever have a brother, the first thing I'll do when he's big enough is have a pillow fight.

"They hung up my chickens by the feet in the butcher shop, and then dumped them in boiling water. Do you like chicken soup?"

At that moment, I didn't care for it.

"You like flowerpots, I remember. And how's your pot doing?"

"Nothing has grown yet," I said sorrowfully. "It's easier to construct a building than to grow radishes."

"It's also easier to fall from a building," said Grandpa, and I was curious to know what was the highest story he'd been to in a skyscraper. He said that there was one building, the Empire State Building, which had more than a hundred stories! I could hardly believe it. It sounded like the Tower of Babel.

"You know how to read English?" asked Grandpa, and he asked me to read to him a long column of numbers from the English newspaper that Daddy brought home for him every evening.

I sat down and read to him but didn't comprehend a single thing.

"That's all?" he asked when I finished. "No more?"

"What are those numbers?" I inquired, and suddenly thought to myself that Grandpa was perhaps a spy. That could also be the explanation for his disappearance.

"They're from the New York Stock Exchange. I worked there after the chicken business."

I wondered whether or not he was proud of his medals.

To me, the word "exchange" sounded fantastic. I was ashamed to admit that I had no idea what it meant. In spite of his explanation about the column of numbers, I didn't give up the possibility of his spying. He didn't realize that I had seen those decorations of honor in the photograph.

I asked, "On what floor did you live?"

"For a short while, on the twenty-eighth floor, but mostly on the third."

I couldn't hide my disappointment. "We have three-story buildings on our street," I said. "And . . . how did you climb up, by the stairs or the elevator? There was an elevator there, right?"

"What do you mean, how did I climb up? By foot!"

"I mean, how did you see where to go?"

"As a blind man, I'm a greenhorn, as they say, not a veteran." A stifled laugh erupted from his throat. "It happened only last year. Soon I'll be just like a baby. They'll take me by the hand and lead me around, one step at a time."

"But you must see something, no? You can't be totally in the dark!"

Grandpa kept quiet.

"Totally dark?" I asked. "Without a single ray of light?"

Grandpa still kept quiet.

"Check out your flowerpot," he spoke at last, "maybe you'll be surprised."

At that moment, I was at a loss about how he knew I had a pot in the first place. I didn't remember telling him about it. Maybe he could really see something, after all.

Maybe at night, when we're blind, his eyes open? And maybe he had magical powers that helped him locate us after he got lost.

I went over to the window to inspect the flowerpot. The circle of earth was flat, smooth, without any hint of growth. They'll never come up, those radishes. I concocted a desperate scheme. A pot is too confining a place. They want a wide bed, something like a field. They weren't interested in my rivalry with the kids on the first floor. Or maybe those seeds had lost themselves in the darkness there. I went back to the porch and asked Grandpa for his newspaper. He didn't ask me why. Turning the pot upside down on the paper, I spread out all the soil. I dug around and fingered the earth in search of the seeds, but the black soil had somehow swallowed them.

I was so busy that I didn't notice when some clods of earth fell from the window and plummeted down. I heard a shriek, as if somebody had a scare. I quickly looked and saw the newly arrived boy standing below my window. He was leaning against a bike but made no attempt to ride it. Looking up at me, he simply stood there and didn't even shake off the cluster of earth from his head. Although I hadn't seen his face on the night they moved in here, I recognized him at once.

My heart began pounding. It bothered me that the ball of earth had to fall on him. Why him and not the others? Why wasn't Avigdor standing there, for example?

But the boy didn't seem angry, only confused. He shook his golden hair and then smiled at me. I waved to him with a hand that was brown and ugly. Small granules of sod stuck into it and hurt. I turned my eyes away from him for a second, and he was gone. Even his bicycle. Vanished. I waited there a while, but he didn't reappear. I went to scrub my hands. Before putting a hand under the faucet, I noticed a seed caught on my middle finger. I carefully replaced it at the bottom of the pot and covered it with a blanket of soil. I thought to myself, so that's how you usually find things—by accident.

7

"Today nobody will be home," Mother said one morning. She shoved me. Ordinarily, she would wake me very gently, stroking my hair or touching my cheek with a soft finger, until my eyes popped open. I had trouble waking in the morning. My head was a sponge full of dreams, and it was hard to let go of them and squeeze the sponge dry. I loved having the tail end of my dreams accompany me all day, till the next night.

Sometimes I'd catch her looking at me in a strange way— with a concentrated expression, as if she were parting from me. After all, I was just going off to school.

That morning, though, she seemed tense and impatient. It was a month or so after Grandpa's arrival.

"Where will you be?" I asked.

Mother said, "We all have to travel someplace."

"What place?"

"Some place. It's not important. . . ."

Adults always say to a child, "It's not important," when they want to conceal something, and it's always the most important thing of all. I learned not to be stubborn about it, since they won't tell you anything if you pressure them. I have my own ways of finding out.

"Will you take the Plymouth?" I inquired.

"Yes. But it's not far away. We'll be back in the afternoon. We have no choice but to give you a key. Know how to use it?"

"Of course," I said. "Don't you remember the day you went to the port . . . to meet Grandpa?"

"Really? I gave you a key?" Suddenly a groove showed on her forehead. "Simha must still have it. Good . . . it's not important."

Again that "it's not important."

They dressed up fancy. In truly marvelous clothes. I couldn't believe it when I saw Mother take her very best dress out of the closet—the one she wore only on Rosh Hashanah and Yom Kippur, and otherwise kept for weddings and Bar Mitzvahs. Except that, since nobody ever invited her to a wedding or Bar Mitzvah, the dress remained just a synagogue outfit. As for Granny, she wore the same elegant clothes she always did—there was no difference.

Mother hurried me. "Well, come on, get cracking! You'll be late for school!"

"But it's still early," I protested.

"Then play with your friends. You need fresh air. In the summer, we'll take you to the beach . . . after everything is worked out. And your appetite will improve, too, and you won't leave all your food on the plate. Did you have a glass of milk yet? You musn't *ever, ever* leave the house on an empty stomach! Why don't you go to school together with Hemda?"

"Hemda isn't my friend; she's just a neighborhood kid. Not everyone who lives next door has to become your friend."

Mother had no patience for fine distinctions. I noticed that she was wearing a string of pearls around her neck. That was her sole jewelry. She said she got it from her mother. My two other grandparents had died at the hands of the Nazis, who made those experiments on Mrs. Starkman, the grocery lady.

"Don't start any arguments now, there's no time for that today," said Mother. "Just hurry up. We have a lot to do."

And that's how they sent me off to school. I didn't even have a chance to check the flowerpot or greet it with a good morning. In the past few days, I decided that you have to really encourage seeds with conversation, too. It certainly couldn't hurt. I felt as if my parents had literally kicked me outdoors. But I didn't leave right away. I hid in the yard of the house next door, behind the shrubs, and saw how Mother helped Grandpa down the stairs, warning him of each coming step. He was wearing a black suit, a tie, and a festive hat on his head. Once Daddy went like that to a funeral, but as far as I knew, it was too early to be burying the dead. So why were they dressed up?

They got into the green Plymouth. Simha peeked out the window and waved to them. "Don't worry," she shouted, "I'll make it on time!" I shrunk below a bush so Simha wouldn't notice me.

Dad was vigorously cleaning the rear window. After

every few scrubs, he'd step back two steps and inspect his work, to see if the glass was shiny enough. But that wasn't all. He began polishing the two chrome fenders on each side. Mother stuck her head out of the window and shouted angrily that they would be late, and it would be very impolite, and you must never keep a rabbi waiting.

A rabbi? All right, so they really were attending a funeral. Quickly, I calculated who might have died. Was anyone sick? But nobody of that sort came to mind. Daddy said, "Okay, fine, I'm finished already." And he got inside the Plymouth. Whenever he turned on the motor, I was sure that the car would pull the same trick she did that Saturday. But since coming out of the mechanic's garage, she behaved like a model car. That Plymouth couldn't complain about anything, because my father treated her like a baby. Every Saturday afternoon, he would carry a bucket and rag downstairs and wash her—it was a special ceremony. All the neighbors would look out their windows at the only automobile on the street.

They drove off, and I walked to school. Slowly—for I had plenty of time. I decided to go down to the end of the block and walk along the Yarkon River when, precisely at that moment, I saw the new boy climb onto his bike. I wanted to call out to him but didn't know his name. I also didn't know where he was headed. He wasn't a student in our school. I began walking faster. My leg muscles tensed. I was practically running. The boy rode his bike on the sand alongside the road. At the far end of the block, they hadn't paved a sidewalk yet. Just yellow sand covered the spaces between the houses. Prickly sand that stuck between your toes. Mother would wring her hands and say, "Again you brought the whole beach into the house." But that sand was completely dry, without shells and without the smell of the sea.

I stepped exactly over the patterns formed by the wheels, and the soles of my shoes smudged the smooth outline. Looking back, I saw the groove we had carved, the bike and I, which looked like a snake of sorts. At the main road, the signature of the wheels suddenly disappeared. I bent over, even gathering up a fistful of golden sand. I felt like a sleuth. But the boy and his bike had vanished. I decided to cross the road. I was afraid I'd be late for school. After I tightened my knapsack, the straps were pressing into my shoulders. It was hot. Summer's around the corner, I mused. How unlucky for them; they had to travel to a cemetery on a day like this, and how unfortunate the dead person was. His whole body must be sweating. So why did Mother wear her best holiday outfit to a funeral? The dead man must be very special. All these thoughts managed to gallop through my head by the time I had reached the other side of the road. I don't know where that bike emerged from, but it suddenly blocked my path. His face looked furious, and his blond hair was strewn over his forehead.

"Girl," he said, "why are you following me?"

I shrank into a ball and kept my eyes on his bicycle wheels. He rocked them back and forth, back and forth, and the track he made in the ground got deeper and deeper.

"I don't like it when anybody follows me. What do you want from me?"

I couldn't utter a word, and just peered from the corner of my eye and watched his blond hair fall over his eyes. My hand had a sudden strange urge. It wanted to brush his hair from his forehead, so I could see the color of his eyes. It was almost ready to move on its own, as if it weren't attached to me.

"Maybe you can't speak Hebrew?" I could hear the mockery in his voice.

"I was simply walking along . . . and I looked at your bike. What's wrong with that? Is that forbidden? I don't have a bicycle. I don't even know how to ride one. Those pedals and that chain . . . it's too complicated for me. And you must balance yourself. I would never succeed at it. . . ."

"Where do you live?"

As I raised my arm, the strap of my knapsack pinched my shoulder. I pointed in the direction of my house.

"Come, get on."

He offered me a hand and pulled me onto the bike. The crossbar cut into my flesh, but that wasn't why my legs were paralyzed. I didn't know what was happening to me.

We rode all the way to school. He knew the route. I was angry at myself. Was this how I should behave? Soon he'll drop you off without a helping hand; he'll just give you a shove. What an embarrassment. That weird sensation in my numb legs, my red-hot cheeks, and that sentence that keeps pounding in my heart over and over: God, God, please let this ride go on forever!

Sometimes he rode with one hand, while the other pushed his blond hair from his forehead. Oh, I wanted so badly to do that for him, since it was dangerous to ride a bike without both hands. At the school gate, he stopped. I almost flew off, my legs tossed into the air. I jumped too quickly for him to offer any help. Now he'll ask me what my name is and then wonder how a girl ever got a boy's name. All surprised, he'll say, Who gave you such a name? And I'll be forced to explain that it comes from someone who was killed by the Nazis, but I don't know exactly who he was. They expected a boy and got a girl, so what could they do? Wait until they might someday have a son? Meanwhile they were obliged to preserve the memory of that Gershon, so they stuck his name onto me. That's what happens to a one-day-old baby, without anyone bothering to ask if she agrees. And what good would it have done if I had screamed "No, no!"?

Right away, he would guess that I was the one the other kids called "Gershona Primadonna." You could hear their screams all the way down to his house.

So I quickly asked him for his, and he paused for a moment, as though he didn't understand my question.

Then the school bell rang. I said, "I have to run!" That's when he said, "Nimrod, call me Nimrod."

All that day, I couldn't stop thinking about him. I was unable to concentrate on my studies. I wanted to rush over to the green blackboard and jump inside. Nimrod with the blond hair and the most wonderful name I had ever heard. Pure Hebrew. They hadn't burdened him with the name of some bygone relative who was nobody to him. I recognized the name Nimrod from the Bible. A hunter. I completely forgot about my family. Their funeral, and their fancy clothes, and their "it's not important." Not until I entered Starkman's Grocery did I remember them, when I heard Mrs. Starkman say to her husband in her quiet Yiddish—she thought I wouldn't understand—"The girl deserves a *mazel tov*. Her grandparents got married again this morning."

40

8

Grandpa and Granny moved out to live together. The apartment seemed empty. I never told anyone that I knew their secret. Deep down, like in that hidden spot where the radish seeds lay, a small pain germinated in my heart. More active than the radishes and quicker to grow. How could it be that I was the only one not invited? What, am I not part of the family? I'm sure they didn't forget silly Aunt Giselle and her bore of a brother Aaron, who used to pinch my cheek while saying with an ear-to-ear grin, "Such a pretty little girl!" And Dudek, who always gave my back a good smack and shouted, "Why haven't you grown? Don't you eat enough vegetables?" Then he'd laugh, too, as if he had just cracked a great joke. Even Simha, who wasn't a relative—only a neighbor and a friend—they hadn't forgotten to invite.

Apparently, it wasn't the custom to invite children to

the wedding of their grandparents—no matter if the grandparents were lost and blind. I also had some very important questions that I couldn't get answered. For example, whether in second marriages you have to break the glass again. And another question bothered me a lot—how did my blind grandfather locate the glass under his shoe? Maybe my father guided him? On second thought, I could be sure that Grandpa made no mistake, for I had proof that he sensed all kinds of things.

They transferred all his belongings to their new quarters. First his brown suitcase, then his suits, together with their hangers, and also his ties, folded perfectly in a nylon bag, and finally his new walking cane. I figured that somebody must have given it to him as a wedding present.

Granny left behind just her sewing kit. I didn't know if that was a sign that she intended to come back some time. Maybe she was sick of embroidering tablecloths with roses. Maybe he told her (now at last he was forced to speak to her) that he wanted another pattern, a thicker one, which he could feel more easily.

I wanted so much to tell someone the secret, but I had nobody. So the following morning, as I was raking those lazy radishes of mine, I whispered it right into the soil. I got so close that my lips were full of earth. At that moment, mother peeked out the kitchen window and began screaming, "Have you lost your mind? The girl is eating dirt!!! What else will you do for your flowerpot? One day I'll throw it out of the house. Worse than a dog."

I began searching for Granny's wedding dress. I made use of the time when Mom was resting and Daddy was at work. I was jealous of my grandmother. She had all the luck. Not just once was she allowed to wear a fantastic white gown, but twice! I know her, she probably considered it nothing unusual, whereas my mother didn't even have a wedding dress for her ceremony, and that's a real pity. I pictured that mysterious costume. A long train in back, and at the cuffs of the sleeves frills and soft wavelets, like frozen foam.

It made me think of those sweet candies that melt in your mouth, called "kisses." My dream is to have a full bag of those candies and devour them in a second. In a store window on Allenby Street, there is a mannequin dressed in a white wedding gown. It has been in that window for years. So gorgeous, no bride would dare wear it.

I ransacked the clothes closets. I even searched the cupboard where all the Passover dishes were kept. Already I knew that adults have strange notions about where to hide things. When Daddy was in America, I discovered one photograph. It was tucked among Mom's nightgowns, in my eyes, the weirdest place to conceal old photographs. I ran to her and told her what I'd found, figuring that it must have wound up there by mistake.

She handled the photograph carefully, as if she feared that it would fall apart in her fingers. The way she gazed at it, I thought this was the first time she'd seen it.

"Who is he?" I asked.

"A boy you don't know."

"Will I ever meet him?"

"I don't think so."

"What was his name?"

It seemed to me that mother's laughter concealed tears. Tears that were ashamed to come out and disguised themselves as laughter instead.

"Do you see his hand?" she asked.

"How can I? He's hiding it behind his back."

"I know what he's holding there."

"What?"

"A bird. He smuggled it into the studio under his coat. The whole time we were afraid it would chirp. He whispered to the bird: *Please don't sing anything now. At least until we've been photographed. Control yourself for a few minutes.*"

"Really just a few minutes?"

Mother turned the photograph over. "We were at the photographer's for at least an hour, and the bird kept quiet. Not even a single peep came out of her. She just fluttered her wings. I heard it. But never mind, I don't like it when you rummage in places you don't belong!"

She took the photograph but didn't put it in the same hiding place under the nightgown. But I didn't forget that boy with his hand behind his back. Now that I was looking for the wedding gown, I remembered that she never revealed his name. Maybe he was the Gershon I was named after. No wonder he was so generous about it. With a name like that! If he had been called Nimrod, he wouldn't have parted with it so easily.

The greatest benefit that I got out of the remarriage of my grandparents was that they moved into Nimrod's building. On the morning before their departure, Grandpa came into my room. Now it was just my room again. The folding bed in the living room was returned to the porch. Grandpa went straight to the window. Again I suspected that he could actually see somewhat. He fingered the air as if it were some delicate fabric.

"Maybe it's too cold for them. This is the northern exposure."

Air escaped from my nose. So here was another expert on plants. Even the gardener couldn't tell me whether the radishes were suffering from some sickness. He said what everybody else said—that I was a girl who had no patience. If I happen to ask a question when they're in a nervous mood, they say I'm a pest. But if an adult keeps asking questions, they say he's very interested, cultured, and curious.

Grandpa suggested, "Perhaps you should move the pot over to our new flat. There the sun lives on the porch on a permanent basis."

I told him it was hard for me to decide. I was afraid the radishes would think that I'd abandoned them and given up all hope for them. I didn't say that it seemed to me that a blind man was incapable of tending a flowerpot. By mistake, he could smash it to smithereens.

"They're not going to make it," I said. "It's hard for me to believe that they'll ever stick their heads out."

"Think it over. Plenty of sunshine. Once they used to think that the sun revolves around the planet earth. Fools. It stands still. Anything that wants to grow has to come closer to it."

"If the buildings in New York are so high up, does that mean they're closer to the sun? Isn't there a danger of catching on fire?"

"If you only knew the view you get from above."

Grandpa sounded like a dreamer. "Everything seems tiny. Hatred disappears, love disappears, all you see are dots racing from right to left, and left to right, up, down, sideways. And the Hudson, the river that circles the city, becomes just a narrow belt. On a clear day, you can see the Statue of Liberty."

"Grandpa," I said, "you're lucky you saw everything before you went blind. Actually, you didn't miss out on anything. You can remember it all. I think it's worse to be born blind. That's like not getting any presents throughout your whole life."

That afternoon, I took the flowerpot over there. I hugged it. The clay was cold. I whispered, "Dear radishes, maybe you'll be better off in another place. Maybe in honor of the remarriage of my grandparents you'll reveal the tip of a leaf." I hope they won't get divorced again. I'm not sure if you can marry a third time.

I climbed the stairs very slowly, calculating each step. All I needed was to fall and smash the pot. What hardships it went through. More than the children of Israel in the desert. It would take us a long time to get upstairs because Grandpa and Granny lived on the third floor—the building's top floor. As I passed by the door on the second floor, I saw that there was no name on it. I stopped for a moment to check if anything was written beside the bell. Then the door opened, and Nimrod stepped out. That was too much for me. I was overcome with shame. I held the pot tightly in my arms and ran down the flight of stairs and bolted from the building.

9

Three days later, a catastrophe happened. Their garden sprouted. Without any prior notice or early warning.

By daybreak, it was covered in a greenish down. It had all happened during the night, but as I was brushing my teeth that morning, I already heard them celebrating. Their screams of excitement hit the sky above. They opened the faucet and hosed everything down. It was so early in the day that nobody had gone to work yet. My faucet went dead, only a few miserable drops dripped out. I ran downstairs to see the disaster with my own eyes. I didn't even drink that glass of milk that was so important to mother ("Never start the day on an empty stomach, because your brain won't work"), or touch the egg whose terrible taste wouldn't leave me alone from breakfast until the ten o'clock recess ("Two eggs a day is crucial. The albumen manufactures the body's cells. Do you realize what difficulties we had three years ago, during the rations? You couldn't even get powdered eggs then—unless you knew somebody!").

I also didn't take my knapsack. I was hoping that Hemda and Avigdor were lying or hallucinating. It just couldn't be true.

They, who never worried about their lousy garden and argued over whose turn it was to water it, who stomped through it in their games of hide-and-seek. And actually dug holes there to play marbles. Yet they were the ones with a garden that grew? What sort of justice was that? Some world!

My flowerpot stood miserable on the windowsill. What tortures it endured, but it still carried on. I was sick and tired of pitying it. I picked it up. All I could think about was smashing it once and for all. It was just a clay shape full of brown earth and boring . . . but they had . . . they had . . . Tears burned my eyes. I considered Grandpa lucky that he was spared this humiliation. He was rid of tears forever. I never learned how to control them; they show up whenever they want and gush nonstop without taking me into consideration. What do they care if everybody laughs at me? Even at school, they'd appear at the most inappropriate moments. In fact, no moment is appropriate for tears. I could be standing at the blackboard struggling to solve a problem in math, and the numbers won't work for me, when those wet blobs start pouring all over me. Or even if I hear kids whispering behind my back and am certain that they're saying "Gershona Primadonna."

Now my tears had a wonderful opportunity and they came gushing. And Mother only added to them as she ran downstairs with my knapsack in one hand and that all-important glass of milk in the other. She shouted that I must finish it at once, otherwise the consequences would be terrible, and that she couldn't take any more of my nonsense because her nerves were weak. I decided to smash the flowerpot; it had given me nothing but grief. Hemda was singing, "My garden, my garden, my dear little garden," directing her song right at me. She was off-key—I was positive. Even the music teacher would excuse her from class and send her out to play in the yard.

I lacked the courage to come closer. I stood in the doorway at the bottom of the stairs—within the shadows—and observed the green stalks as if they were my enemies. The entire street was yellow with sun and sand. There were still only a few houses around. I prayed for a sudden gust of wind to cover those stalks with a heap of dust. My mouth still tasted of toothpaste, even after I drank Mom's glass of milk. At school, I imagined the sun scorching everything that had grown during the night. When they would return home, they'd find all their stalks and stems burned yellow and utterly wilted.

Avigdor announced that he was inviting the whole class to a "gardenwarming" ceremony. He explained that it would be just like a housewarming. Many children understood what he meant. There wasn't a kid who hadn't moved from one place to another, or arrived from somewhere else. The whole housing project was under construction. Every day another tractor came to level another vacant lot, and the construction workers stood on high scaffolds without the least fear of falling. Daddy explained to Grandpa that the entire country would soon be covered with housing projects and the transit camps would disappear, so the new immigrants who were arriving in hordes could finally find a "roof over their heads after all their hardships." That's what Daddy said. Grandpa answered that you had to be careful not to overcrowd the place.

Hemda said to me with a show of generosity, "Gershona, you can come to the gardenwarming, too, if you want. You may find it worth a look, you might also have a garden someday." Meanwhile, they fenced in the flower bed with the popsicle sticks they had saved all year, the ones with letters on them. If you put together all the letters of the word *popsicle,* you won some sort of prize. I stopped collecting them after I realized that you could never get the letter C. I was amazed that they had used up their gigantic stockpile. Starkman himself would give them any discarded sticks he found near the grocery. For such a collection, they could surely trade for at least twenty pictures of movie stars or soccer players.

The whole flower bed was underwater. Avigdor assigned each child a turn to use the hose. The yard turned into a rainy season of winter puddles. Only the neighboring lot escaped drenching. With its mounds of sand, it always remained dry. The kids' shoes got splattered with mud, and the whole section of the sidewalk in front of the house was a jumble of foot and shoe prints. Luckily Granny wasn't living here anymore, otherwise she would be screaming at them, "Barbarians!"

Hemda went over to Avigdor and whispered something in his ear. Pointing the hose at me, he said, "Want a turn?" Meanwhile, he directed the nozzle right at my legs and blasted me. Without saying he was sorry, he lowered the hose so the water would drench my sandals, too. Nevertheless, I took my turn. And splashed the stalks, wishing in my heart that they would drown. I was their rain, their storm, their harshest winter. You could already sail paper boats in that garden. It reminded me of a documentary short I once saw before a feature film. They showed how rice was planted in China. The Chinese stood up to their knees in water, yet weren't afraid of sinking. It was astounding to see the amount of water they had in China, while here our teacher would ask us to record in our notebooks: "Never waste a drop of water." Just our luck, we settled in a land where the sun was its most significant tenant. In China the sun visits only from time to time, and doesn't manage to swallow all the water. I remembered that Grandpa said the sun resided on their porch. He couldn't see its light anymore, but its heat made even a blind man suffer.

Ignoring Avigdor's indications that there was a long line behind me, I wouldn't let go of the hose. I had my own plan—to drown those miserable stalks. Then I pitied them. How were they to blame? Imagine that you are this seedling—just a baby, my heart told me. You were born just last night, and already today somebody is soaking you in water nonstop, until you can't breathe. And you figure that the world you entered is nothing but a pool or a vast ocean. I thought that if I persisted in playing the role of rain, they would wonder if they were fish and not plants. So I returned the hose to Avigdor, saying, "Thanks a lot." I drew my legs out of the puddle and looked for some dry spot. I realized that I had to dry them out before going back upstairs, otherwise Mom might go crazy with anger. Avigdor said, "If you care to water tomorrow, too, you can . . . oh, here comes your father!"

Daddy was busy parking the car. It always took a long time for him to attach her exactly to the curbstone. When he came home, the passersby would all stop and gawk. A car like that they saw only in the movies. They must have thought we were rich. But we never travelled far with her, not even to Jerusalem. We didn't know anybody in Jerusalem. Daddy said that he loved his Plymouth but she was too big for him. For Americans, he said, the car was fine— huge like the country itself, which was endless. But in our land, which is both tiny and poor and only ten years old, in our land the Plymouth was a stranger. When they would talk about how young the state was, he would tell me "She is even younger than you are," as though I had to look out for her like an older sister.

All the children forgot about the garden ceremony and raced over to look at the Plymouth. Daddy apparently got nervous about the mob of kids stampeding toward him and parked poorly. The car jolted onto the vacant lot next door, and the wheels sunk into sand. Daddy tried to free her, but the more he pressed the gas pedal, the more the wheels spun in place and sprayed dirt in all directions. In the battle between Daddy and the wheels, Daddy lost. I was furious at the Plymouth for causing us another humiliation, but Daddy looked unworried. "Come on, kids, I need your help," he said, and all of us lined up behind the green Plymouth and shoved. Avigdor stood on the sidelines and shouted, "Heave ho! Heave ho!" and he swung the empty hose. Hemda ran to the end of the line and heaved all she could. Then she switched places and stood right in back of me. I felt her hands pushing me. "If the car won't be able to go anywhere, we can always push it. It'll be like a stroller for babies," said Hemda.

We pushed hard, but only on the third try did the Plymouth free itself. Boy, how heavy she was, a real elephant. She rocked from side to side. Two boys pounced on her back and rode like that, grabbing her flashy fenders. Now they ruined the shine that Daddy had worked so hard to achieve. Even some mud stuck to her from the soles of their shoes, the stuff left over from their hours of afternoon work in the new garden.

When Daddy extended his hand to me to escort me home, I saw Mom standing there watching us. She had just returned from work. A loaf of bread and four glass bottles of yogurt rested in her string shopping bag.

"You're making a fool of yourself with that car. You didn't have to bring it along with you in the first place," she said.

"And should I have brought back my father, do you think?"

Mother bent her head. Daddy took the bag from her hand. In it there was also a green cluster bursting with red-violet lumps.

Mom said, "I got you something. You love radishes, I know. But it's not the season now. Still, I found the last ones at the greengrocer's. We can put them in a salad. I hope they won't be too sharp." I was too shy to hug her in front of the other kids. I didn't want Mom and Dad to hear what they call me. It would grieve them to know what the children made of the name they had chosen for me. It would sadden them to realize that nobody had any respect for the memory of their Gershon.

The next day, after school, I finally decided to transfer the flowerpot to Grandpa's apartment. It would be the last chance for both of us. If it wouldn't grow there, it wouldn't grow anywhere. And as for me, I would never again so much as attempt to grow any other plant from seed.

10

He smiled at me. His blond hair was combed and didn't fall in his eyes. "It's you."

Lucky me, he didn't know my name. Maybe he wouldn't put the two of us together. "Who are you bringing that pot to?"

"It's *my* pot."

"But it's empty. I mean, it just has soil—"

"Not so. I planted . . . flowers in it. A rare kind. They grow only in desert heat. There are such flowers."

"So maybe we should put it on the roof? What do you say? That's the hottest spot in the building."

We climbed upstairs. The roof was bathed in blinding light. I had to lower my eyelids to see anything clearly. I thought to myself, is that how a blind person feels, except without the heat?

We searched for the right location. We checked the rays

of sunshine from every angle. I fingered the air, the way Grandpa does, to determine the temperature. I felt like a weather forecaster, though they make mistakes sometimes, too.

In the end, Nimrod selected the appropriate spot—near the edge of the roof, by the laundry room. He set down the pot, inspected it from all sides, stepping back and forth like that time with his bike.

"Right here. There's a kind of little wall to protect it. The Cohen family's cat walks here at night. I can hear him leaping."

"Aren't you afraid it might be a thief?"

"What's there to steal from us? I pity the crook who robs us. After all his troubles, he'll leave poorer than he entered."

"Why does a flowerpot need a wall? Who would want to steal it?"

"You'd be surprised. Sometimes a wall is absolutely necessary. It's a pity, though, that anybody on the other side of the wall won't see your flowers. Usually it's the opposite."

"How do you know so much about walls? Some expert . . ."

Nimrod chuckled. Strange. He had the same laugh as Mother. Tears in disguise, but both Mother and Nimrod had control over their droplets, and I still had much to learn from them.

"How come you picked this building in particular? Haven't you got a roof or a porch?"

"My grandpa moved in here. He and his wife . . . they're the new tenants in the building."

"The man who . . . can't see? He's your grandfather?"

He was truly a well-mannered boy. Granny would be amazed at the way he carefully chose his words to avoid saying that awful word, *blind*. What would he say if he knew that, in my heart, I also call him "lost"?

We shifted into the shade. It was hard to breathe in such heat. Nimrod straddled his legs over two separate steps and leaned on his bent knee. He looked at me through the screen of hair in front of his face and didn't speak. It was difficult to part, but whether from him or the flowerpot, I couldn't decide. Already I was waiting for that gesture of his—his fingers brushing away his stubborn hair. It didn't stay combed for long. All sorts of strands of hair, in smooth clusters, continually tossed every which way.

"I'll let you know if anything grows. Every day I'll come up here to the roof and check. And also . . . if you wish, I could water it."

I wondered what would happen if he discovered that I hadn't planted flowers inside? He would consider me a liar. Anyway, he'll find out what they call me and join them. Simha's explanation of the word *primadonna* hadn't satisfied me, and I'd gone and looked it up in a dictionary. What it said was "first lady." So what was so insulting about being a first lady? In the dictionary, it sounded rather honorable. With some words, though, what counts is not what they mean but how they're spoken. Even the words *sweet Gershona* would sound like an insult the way Hemda and Avigdor would say them.

I wanted to ask him who gave him such a beautiful name and tell him how fortunate he was, but the words remained buried inside me.

He asked, "Will you come here every day?"

"My grandpa is pretty lonely. He has no friends at all. He doesn't know anybody in the whole country."

"Is he a new immigrant, then?"

"Yes," I said. "Do you know any old immigrants?"

"But people were living here before we arrived," said Nimrod.

"Too bad I can't get to know them. I don't even know where to start looking."

"When you grow up, you'll be able to find all sorts of people, if you remember to."

"I think I'll remember. My grandfather . . . you know, he never forgot Granny after many, many years. In my family, we know how to remember."

"In mine, we want to forget." Nimrod lowered his head and kicked the step. Even that reminded me of my mother.

"Will you be here tomorrow?"

"Right after school. I'll be thinking about the flowerpot all day. It's a great idea to plant flowers. I can't wait for them to bloom."

"And if . . . just leaves grow? Will you be angry?"

"I never get angry. I told you—in my family we want to forget. I could also visit your grandfather. I don't have a grandfather of my own. I'd accept even a . . . blind one."

A neighbor came upstairs with a basket of laundry. She scolded us. "You're blocking the way." We began descending the stairs. I stopped by Grandpa's door, and Nimrod went on. At the bend, he turned around. "You won't forget?"

Without saying a word, I nodded my head while my heart leaped inside me.

I rang twice, knowing they were at home—where could they go? Where could Granny take him, to Simha's? Who said Simha had to be Grandpa's friend—just because she was Granny's best friend? I heard them arguing over who should open the door. Grandpa insisted that he wanted to do it, and Granny grumbled, "You'll only bump into something and break your neck. That's all I need now." At least now I had proof that they talked to each other when they were alone together.

As I entered, he asked, "You found a new friend?"

"He's not a friend," I said, "just somebody. He has a bike."

"That's good, a bicycle. You'll take biking trips. Your mother will finally allow it. Your grandmother considers it improper to converse on the staircase. Everybody can hear you. So you'll visit us every day?"

His eyes were shut. He groped around to find me and managed to touch my shoulder. He had a large hand, but soft. He didn't wish to cause any pain to those chickens he plucked for their feathers, even though they were already dead.

I, too, closed my eyes and listened only to his voice. On the inside, I felt as if I were asking for something, even begging, but I didn't know exactly what it was.

Granny hushed him. "What are you nagging the girl about? You're just confusing her. Better she should eat something and do her homework the way it ought to be done, instead of gallivanting outside. And you encourage her yet to go on excursions? Don't you realize that the sun in this country is dangerous, especially for children? It's a pity you can't see how the girl is dressed. Rags. Nothing more. Khaki pants you call an outfit for a girl? One day I'll make you a dress, as it should be!"

Grandpa opened his eyes and glowered at her with those irises of his. They were transparent and bright. I stood with my mouth open, convinced that he could see. Something, maybe not every detail, but some sort of picture. And maybe on very special occasions when it was crucial for him to see everything, his eyes overcame their handicap.

"Why are you looking at me like that? What did I say? I know that girl from the day she was born. And I know what's good for her. You'll tire out your weak eyes." Grandpa didn't even blink.

Granny shrugged her shoulders. "All right. Let it be your way. Keep turning the girl's head around. If not, you'd have nothing else to do."

I waited for her to leave, then I asked, "Grandpa, what is it like living in the dark?" (Is it altogether black, or just dark gray? and maybe sometimes a stubborn beam of light smuggles inside anyway. Maybe blind eyes are like shutters. You can't ever close them completely tight, a thin strip of light manages to penetrate somehow.)

He said, "It's a hallway, what the English call a corridor. Repeat after me—cor-ri-dor." I repeated after him. And became an echo.

"Blindness is being in a very narrow corridor. Confining, confining. You can't imagine it, or maybe you can? You're still a girl, but you have the intelligence of an adult. And occasionally children possess the imagination that grown-ups have forgotten. In that corridor, you need a lot of imagination. How come you have no sisters or brothers?

60

What are they waiting for, your parents? Don't they understand what little time is left?"

Afterward, he again asked me to read the New York Stock Exchange to him. He said that my father did it as a duty but not with any joy, whereas I read with all my heart, even if I didn't understand what I was reading.

"What's a stock exchange?" I asked.

"A place where people buy and sell paper slips."

"Papers, you mean napkins? That's something I really know about. I have a collection of napkins. Daddy brought me a bunch of them from America."

"Yes. He always asked for them in restaurants. That's when he told me about you for the first time. I gave him all the napkins I had in the house. I hope you're pleased. And I'll keep saving them for you. The Exchange doesn't use paper for packing or writing. Each slip stands for something big, say a house, say real estate or a factory."

"Is it a game? But if you don't live there anymore, how can you still play?"

"They think that if I have no eyes, I don't know how to buy or sell, what's going up or down. You could explain to them that even in a narrow corridor a person is able to find a corner to rest his legs."

Suddenly I felt the need to say a good word about darkness. Now I realized that he would never emerge from his corridor, that I was just deceiving myself into thinking he could see something. I told him that I sometimes love darkness. Not all darkness—just what's under the blanket. I said that I called it a "tent," and that maybe one day Mother would allow me to go on a hike. All these years, she refused, even when the teacher herself came over to ask her personally. Mother said she couldn't bear it, maybe later when I was a bit older, after my Bat Mitzvah. She begged me not to be angry at her, on account of her weak nerves, but I was angry anyway. I was the only one in the whole class who stayed home. "Even dogs go on walks," I told Grandpa.

"I'm sure she'll change her mind. This is your year for hiking. I'll talk to her about it. Walking a dog is something simple. What can happen to a dog?"

"Do you know who Leika is?" I asked. "That's the dog the Russians sent out into space in a sputnik. I always think about her. Why haven't they returned her to earth after she completed their mission for them? Just imagine, Grandpa, Leika is travelling in a tiny spaceship. She's cramped and cold, and she circles the earth over and over again. . . . Do you think Leika's dead?"

Grandpa didn't answer right away. It was a difficult question. He pondered it.

As he leaned his back against the wall, his thoughts concentrated on the tip of his walking stick. Instead of gesturing with his hands, he drew circles with his cane, like Leika's revolutions.

"Do you remember the word I taught you?"

"Cor-ri-dor."

"Leika is sitting in a flying corridor," said Grandpa. "It's true that darkness surrounds her, but I don't think that she's sad. You understand, there's a difference. My corridor is on earth, but Leika is soaring up in heaven, which is something altogether different—because there they never turn off the lights!"

11

In less than a week, the garden put forth buds. It was still impossible to tell what flower would finally emerge from each bud, but their heads were already visible, clearly haughty flowers, matching in character those who had planted them.

Simha sat by the window all day, making sure that nobody lifted a foot to trample them, heaven forbid. Hemda prepared signs with the name of each flower, and in honor of the occasion, the teacher devoted an entire class to "Flowers of Our Land." On Saturday, the class went to "Anemone Hill." Anemones grew there only in the winter, but the name stuck even in summer. Now the hill was covered with gentians, and the children ran around plucking them. I didn't care that much for gathering flowers, because I noticed that they barely last half a day in a glass and then wither overnight. Hemda announced that whatever grew on the hill didn't compare to her own beautiful flowers. The teacher seated us in a circle and explained the difference between a wildflower and a cultivated one. "Cultivated," she said, "is a synonym for trained." The kids complained about the heat, while I imagined a circus of flowers where some flower trainer lashed them with his whip and forced them to step across a thin wire.

The whole neighborhood came to see the new garden. Our house turned into a unique phenomenon. Both a car and a garden—nothing but the best! Even the gardener who'd given me the radish seeds showed up. I pulled him aside and notified him that there wasn't a single sign of life in my flowerpot.

"In a pot?" he burst out laughing. "You planted radishes in a flowerpot?" My head drooped.

"That's no home for vegetables. You're really funny. Everything needs the right home. Even people can't be dragged just anywhere."

"Yes, they can," I said angrily. "I know somebody who moved here from America and adjusted very nicely."

The moment I said it, I knew it wasn't true. Granny hadn't adjusted to her first and second husband, her new-old one. She was concerned about him—that I saw for myself. She followed all his instructions, and he had quite a few—in which sequence to hang his ties and exactly how much starch to use for his shirt collars. She did it all, but without any joy. She went out with him on regular walks every day, even though she grumbled about the flies and other insects along the Yarkon that attacked her delicate skin. The devil take them, she said.

She hooked her arm in his. He leaned on his cane, and

64

off they went, but nobody said about them that they were a pair of lovebirds. Most of their time together they were silent, and it made no difference that they had shared thirty-five years of memories.

Now I had two homes. Every day after school, I would go directly to them. The person who was happiest over this arrangement was Starkman, since he could now count on Mom's services till the moment he closed up his shop.

I would wait for the final bell, and Grandpa would also be waiting for it. He knew by heart my schedule of classes—when I had Bible, geography, and the algebra I hated. On Friday, he never forgot to ask me if I had dropped any coins into the blue "Jewish National Fund" box because there were too many bald hills in our country. How do you know? I asked him. After all, Daddy didn't drive him anywhere in his Plymouth.

Grandpa always had his newspaper ready. My school wasn't far from home. Maybe he heard the bell from his room—if his radio wasn't on. From America, he brought the biggest radio I had ever seen. A square box with eight lamps, two loudspeakers, and a circular antenna that prevented almost any static disturbance. A radio that had both short and medium waves. As Grandpa explained all its marvellous features, his eyes opened and sparkled. It had four knobs, like two sets of eyes, and a fabric that felt like waves when you touched it while you listened.

Grandpa pressed up against it, all the while switching stations and listening to all sorts of voices from far-off lands. In the afternoon he would listen to the "Bureau for Missing Relatives," a program that catered to those who were still looking for their family members lost during the

Nazis' time and never seen again. Although the great war ended before I was born, this program was on every day. There was one Abramov family that kept broadcasting information to a certain Abraham for months on end. Sarah and Yankel Abramov didn't give up hope. Each time they altered their message a bit, but always ended with the words "We're waiting for you."

Once I even found Simha listening to this station on her radio, which was considerably less fancy than Grandpa's. Maybe she was hoping that her deceased would air the news of his longing for her.

The door was already open. Granny was dusting with a stick bedecked with multicolored feathers. I asked her to save it for Purim, so I could dress up as an Indian squaw and call myself, for one day, "Little Feather." "Why not as a ballerina?" asked Granny, disappointed, offering to make me a special dress out of pure linen.

As usual, I took the newspaper from the shelf to read Grandpa the New York Stock Exchange page, but he said that today it wasn't necessary. I asked why.

"Because your father was here last night and already read it to me."

"Don't you want to hear it again?"

Grandpa closed the door. "Today tell me what you look like."

"Me? I'm a typical girl."

"Are you tall? Thin, like your grandmother says? Pale or tanned? What sort of a nose do you have?"

I touched my nose. I'd never thought about it. "A regular nose," I said, "which can smell and, in winter, sneezes a lot."

"And what does your grandmother look like?"

I wrinkled my forehead. "She's not tall. Her skin is the color of milk, and she has lines around her eyes, which are gray . . . I think, like her hair. Which she wears in a bun on her neck. How did she used to look?"

Grandpa drew himself up in his chair. "I don't remember."

I insisted. "Was her hair brown or blond? Did it fall across her forehead and cover her eyes so she had to brush it away with her hand?" Grandpa went back to his radio, turning the knobs quickly until he found a station that aired the news in English.

"Do the Americans also have a Bureau for Missing Relatives?" I asked.

He answered, "They never got displaced. They were lucky." Then he turned off the radio and faced me.

"What does your father look like?"

"Like . . . like . . . Daddy."

He nodded his head. "I realize that."

"You don't remember him either?"

"Come closer to me," he asked, leaning back. I stood in front of him and he put out his fingers and felt my face. I didn't budge. His fingers touched my nose, brow, cheeks, passing onto my lips and hovering over my ears and lobes. He measured the length of my braids, and during all this I didn't make a move. I barely dared to breathe. "Now I can see you," he said finally and touched my nose again. "What does it smell?"

"Whatever people try to conceal." I wanted to laugh, but the voice that came out of me didn't sound like laughter.

"Do you resemble your father or mother?"

I shrugged my shoulders. "Some say one thing and others say the exact opposite. Nobody agrees on who I look like. But my name . . . I'm the only person with such a name. . . . Will you allow me to see you now?"

Grandpa brought his face close to me, and I touched his nose, mouth, ears, and the area where his hair started growing on his forehead. His eyes I didn't dare touch. When I stopped he said, "You didn't see everything." And he placed my hand on his eyes. The lashes tickled. He opened his eyes wide, and I gazed directly into his pupils and saw myself. Shivers shook my back.

"So how do I look to you?"

I stammered. "You . . . you look like my father."

Grandpa covered his face in his two hands. "I'm tired," he said, "go back home."

Granny entered. "Did something happen?" Her apron was soiled, and she dried her hands nervously on it. "Why did you shut the door?"

She escorted me to the door and whispered, "You're right. They really do look alike. . . ."

I couldn't leave before making sure of something first. "Do you think I hurt his feelings?" Granny's hug surprised me.

"You're the one thing he looks forward to."

"Because I read him the New York Stock Exchange page?"

"Now go," said Granny, and her voice was choked. I thought she was going to kiss me, and I waited, but she went back inside and wrapped herself in the apron as if she were cold.

68

I was really confused. I walked slowly, and nothing could break through the heavy wall of my thoughts, not even the bus that flushed me with a cloud of smoke. The workers on the scaffold waved to me as usual, but I couldn't respond. It was strange. When Daddy and Grandpa were in separate places, it was hard to see any similarity between them, but when they were together—it hit you, it was so obvious. The atmosphere was always tense then. I noticed that Grandpa wouldn't open his eyes when Daddy was in the room. On the contrary, he shut them tight on purpose. And two sets of wrinkles fanned out across his temples. Daddy, too, was different from the father I knew. He lost his cheerfulness and didn't tell any of the stories he thought were funny. To make him happy, I would laugh even when there was nothing to laugh at. I was uncomfortable in the company of both of them. I sought excuses to leave the room, but they insisted that I stay put. Sometimes they spoke to each other through me. They didn't touch each other, and they never hugged so much as once. Maybe the hug of greeting at the port was enough for them. Maybe Grandpa hadn't managed to answer all the questions, and Daddy was left with a few unsolved riddles that he couldn't figure out.

The street was quiet—the lull of afternoon. I was amazed that he said he couldn't remember Granny when she was younger. How can people forget what they must remember?

Near Hemda and Avigdor's garden, the children were swarming again. I halted instantly. I didn't want to bump into them. I just stood still, waiting for them to disperse. Luckily they were already on their way home. Hemda said good-bye to them, promising a round of watering turns for tomorrow, and Mrs. Rosen, her mother, screamed that her afternoon meal was getting cold. All the windows of my house stared at me. White empty eyes. Like those glass eyes of Grandpa's, save for the shiny pupils. Even Simha had abandoned her post and taken a nap. The yard was empty, the rubber hose lay curled up in a coil. I stepped on it angrily. Something wild burst out of me—a horse bolting from the stable and running amok on purpose. The snobbish buds swayed in front of me with their closed faces. I squinted. The windows were still empty. I walked right into the garden, and my feet crushed every stalk they encountered along the way. The wild horse reared inside me and neighed, and with every neigh of his, I squashed another shoot, and some I pulled up, root and all. The soles of my sandals were covered in green dough. It was a glorious feeling. My victory was total. No more humiliation. I had demolished the garden that had blossomed just to spite me. The garden that neither sun nor rain could destroy, that two kids on the first floor were so proud of, though only I knew that they didn't give a hoot for what they were growing. Again I stomped on the stalks and they toppled easily. I even jumped on them. That's it, all done! They won't trouble me anymore. Good-bye garden, good-bye shame. If I had the name Gershona, then I might as well be a primadonna!

My victory suddenly went sour. In its place came a wave of terror. What had I done? screamed the horse and ran into hiding in the darkest corner of the stable. I began moving backward. The garden looked like a man who had been punched in the face. The uprooted stalks burned my

70

hand. As I backed off, I didn't take my eyes off the gaping wound in the heart of the flower bed. A few buds were left, but to me they seemed crushed, too.

I didn't know what to do with my sandals. I was afraid to turn on the faucet, in case Hemda and Avigdor might hear it and come outside to see what was going on. Where could I run to? I rushed to the adjacent lot and climbed the small mound of sand. My legs sunk in the sand almost to my knees, but I pushed on farther and farther. I sat down on the slope and vowed never to go near that flower garden again.

As I climbed down, I heard the sound of a bicycle. Nimrod was pedalling forcefully, and in one hand, he held my knapsack.

"Your grandmother sent me to give it back to you," he shouted. "You forgot it!" His bike halted.

"What are you holding?" asked Nimrod, with curiosity.

The torn stalks were on fire. I waited for the chance to rid myself of them. Please let him not look at the garden and see what I had done there. Otherwise, he'll turn his back on me in disgust. I couldn't bear that. Hemda and Avigdor's anger was one thing, but Nimrod's scorn was quite another matter. . . .

Blocking the garden from view with my body, I quickly stuffed the stalks into my knapsack. I prayed that he would go home now. "Don't you have anything to do?" I barked.

"What happened to you today?" He sounded wounded. "I thought you'd be glad to see me. I raced right from school. I thought . . . that you . . ." He swivelled his bike around and rode off in a hurry. I called after him to stop, but he continued speeding in the direction of the

Yarkon River and showed no signs of having heard me.

All the windows of the house looked down on me with sightless eyes that saw each mistake a child or adult ever makes. My heart told me it's a lucky thing that Grandpa hadn't seen it. That night, I dreamed that the windows closed in on me. Each window became a gaping mouth screaming at me, "Monster! Creep! Plant abuser! Anything beautiful that you see you must destroy!" Nimrod had a role in the nightmare, too. His face flared in every window and his voice sounded very close, literally in my ear. "You deserve the name Gershona!"

The following morning, when I opened my knapsack in class, the seedlings that I had uprooted peered out at me. They had wilted, and their necks were broken. The buds were shrunken. As was I, knowing that they would never have the opportunity to bloom.

12

For three days, I quaked with fear. I was sure suspicion would fall on me. Who else did Avigdor hate so much? And Hemda would not have missed a chance to get me in trouble. I swore I would deny it; I would say I spent the whole afternoon with my grandparents. Me? I didn't even go near the garden! I would lie without batting an eyelash.

Nimrod was the only one who could expose me. But I hadn't see him for three days in a row. His shutters were closed. On the third day, his bike was parked at the entranceway. I was certain he was isolating himself indoors, and I didn't call out to him. When I went upstairs to the roof, for my daily visit, I saw that somebody had already tended the flowerpot. The soil was wet. Despite his anger at me, he wouldn't take it out on the pot. He had set up a small awning for it and had rested the pot on a brick he'd gotten from the construction workers on the scaffold.

I knew he came home from school at least an hour after I did. I used to go out onto Simha's veranda to keep an eye on the house at the far end of the block. First I'd spy a cloud of dust approaching and then the bike cruising zigzag. He made figure eights and did other tricks, and I'd smile. Sometimes I had the feeling he knew I was spying, but I didn't care. When he rode without hands, my breath stopped. In any case, something strange happened to my breathing whenever I saw him—I'd swallow air as if I were drinking water.

Most of the day, Nimrod was by himself. His father worked at the Tel Aviv port and would come home late. Nimrod took care of himself, did all his own shopping at the market and never once would consent to buying on credit, in spite of my mother's and Starkman's assurances that he could. A small basket was attached to his bike, and the bottles of yogurt would clink when he came to a stop. He even cooked for himself and cleaned house. Once I saw him beating a carpet whose texture was all gone and whose colors had faded; it reminded me of the only carpet we had, which was in our living room. The story goes that when Granny emigrated to Israel, she carried it rolled under her arm, and when the British boarded their ship, she refused to be separated from the rug, and even smacked a British soldier on the head for daring to inquire what it was. How I laughed at that tale! To this day, I can't believe it really happened.

Nimrod and I met in the stairwell or on the roof. He never once invited me to his apartment and I never asked. For three days, I waited for him, reconstructing in my mind the way I'd stood opposite him, with those crushed stalks in my hand. Although I tried to conceal them from him, I was now convinced he had actually seen them.

Hemda and Avigdor conducted a thorough investigation of the vandalism done to their garden, and they came to the conclusion that the perpetrator of the crime against the seedlings was . . . a dog. I had a good laugh. Luckily they knew nothing about footprints. Since when does a dog wear shoes?

I could breathe easy now. One of the two stones on my chest rolled off. I had no more interest in their garden. They could choke together with their flowers. Even so, I enjoyed seeing the garden recover and regain all its former colors. Small buds transformed into chrysanthemums and dahlias and snapdragons and also short pansies, which I especially loved. I passed by the flower bed twice a day without any envy for one reason alone: Their garden existed and so did my Nimrod.

On the fourth day, I decided to wait for him at his door, which still had no name. I sat there on bended knees and waited. I heard doors opening and closing. Neighbors who came up the stairs looked at me curiously but didn't say a word.

I recognized his footsteps immediately.

"Are you still angry at me?"

He shrugged his shoulders. "You don't owe me anything."

"I didn't really mean it. You understand . . . their garden . . . it blossomed."

He shook his hair. "Why haven't you any patience?"

"Do you think plants communicate with each other?" I asked. "Do they talk to one another or something?"

"I have no idea."

I tried again. "For example, if somebody damages a plant, do you think another plant, that's growing somewhere far away, knows about it?"

Nimrod said, "It depends if plants are like people. People can sense what's happening to somebody else even when they're far away from them."

At once I thought of Grandpa and Granny. "If that's the case, then my flowerpot will never sprout anything."

"I don't think plants snitch," said Nimrod, pulling me after him to the roof. Together we raked the soil in the pot and refrained from catching each other's eye. He went to get some water in a funnel, and I tried to be very busy. Something inside me wanted to run away, but another part of me wanted me to stay.

When we parted, I felt as though I'd been bewitched by a magician who planted inside me a shiny warm seed that moved as I moved and also made music. Nimrod didn't call me by my name, and that was reason enough to love him. Another secret sank into me, to keep company with the closeted photograph of the boy and Granny's wedding dress. But there was a difference now. The other secrets had thorns, whereas Nimrod's became a magic seed. What was really strange was that even though I felt miserable, I was happy. I couldn't understand how that was possible. Perhaps I am similar to Granny that way. When I pronounced Nimrod's name, it sounded magical. It was enough for me to whisper it to my heart and the seed would start shifting around and sprouting warm branches and my whole body would tingle and ring.

Granny made sure that Grandpa had his daily walk. His

mood deteriorated. He complained about food, the torrid, annoying country, and boredom. He spoke longingly of his city with the tall towers. Whenever I read him the Stock Exchange numbers, he would relax in the armchair, enjoying it as though I were reciting poetry. The skin on his face put on a gray hue and sometimes looked transparent. Blue veins showed around his eyes. Daddy took him to one doctor and then another doctor who lived in Jerusalem. They drove there in the Plymouth and came back looking more grieved than when they left. Daddy told Mother that an operation wouldn't help because his blindness was terminal. During these days, Grandpa opened his eyes less and less, and the color in his pupils wasn't always clear. Only when I would come traipsing up the steps and throw my knapsack by the doorway and shout, "Here I am!" would a light shine in his face, and Granny would rejoice at seeing me. Living with us, she hadn't hugged me as many times as she did once she moved in with her own husband. But she always had her pet warning: "Wipe your feet. You're bringing all your sand into the house." And it didn't help if I explained that we just had physical education and practiced broad jumps in sandboxes.

"Well, you should only be healthy." She was always wishing me health as though we lived in a hospital.

One day she was sick, and I offered to take her place on their daily stroll. It was two weeks before our summer vacation. I asked Grandpa where he would like to walk, and he answered, "To the Yarkon. She never takes me there. Your grandmother loves to stroll on your unpaved streets. A park to her is the garden outside the clinic. Just old-timers sit there. I can't bear them."

I followed her example, though, hooking my arm in his, exactly the way she does. He grabbed his cane and called out to the bedroom, "Regina, we're going!"

"I ask that you be very careful with him," she called back.

"She thinks I'm a baby," grumbled Grandpa. "Have you got the key?"

I took him downstairs slowly and didn't pinch him with my fingers like she does. I indicated in advance when each step and each turn in the staircase was coming.

"Is the Yarkon a big river?"

"My teacher calls it a stream."

"Now describe everything to me. Don't skip anything. Every person we meet, every house, every tree. You be my eyes."

"Does Granny do that, too?"

"She tries. But she doesn't always succeed. She misses things. Who's the man approaching us?"

"It's the mailman."

Grandpa said, "So let's wait for him." The mailman removed a bundle of letters from the blue bag hanging from his shoulder and turned to us. "Do you live here?"

Grandpa stood erect. "I'm from the third floor. Do you have a letter for me? From America?"

The mailman riffled through the bundle and shook his head no. Grandpa was disappointed.

"I have a letter for somebody named Janek Orlovski, but I don't see that name on any of the mailboxes."

I took the letter for a moment. It had a bunch of foreign stamps on it. The address was correct.

"There's nobody with that name in our building. It must be the wrong address."

As we headed out, he was still holding the letter.

We went down to the very banks of the river. Grandpa wanted to touch the water, and I also dipped my hand into it. The water was cool and the current gentle. I looked deep inside to see if any fish were there. I remembered that in the river by Hadera, there once were crocodiles. But that was before I was born. A tangle of bulrushes blocked the shoreline. I told Grandpa we called them "rushes" and made kites from them.

"What?"

"Kites. We tie them together with a string and fly them in the wind. They always get caught in the trees."

Grandpa asked me to cut him a bulrush for a memento, but he didn't have a pocketknife. The reed was tough and wouldn't break. We entered the vegetation. The grasses were tall and dense. I held onto his hand tightly, so he wouldn't slip in the mud along the bank or trip on a stone. We reached the dock for the boats. On Saturday, we sometimes went to Reading Beach. One day, they will build an electric generator there. Meanwhile, the only thing there was a wooden bridge, a shaky one at that, and a narrow strip of beach with enormous waves and a raging surf.

I told him how Mother had taken me to the sea when I was young because she believed that the "sea stimulates the appetite." I explained that actually I was terrified of the water and didn't want to disturb the big animal with white teeth that came at me and, only at the last moment, pulled back. Grandpa told me what New York looked like to him the first time he saw it thirty-five years ago. At home, in Poland, he had left behind a wife and a small baby, who today is my father. He didn't say why he had left them. After three months of an ocean voyage, the ship neared the harbor. He saw Ellis Island and the Statue of Liberty, which was a stone woman with horns on her head and a torch in her hand. All the immigrants pressed against the boat railing and broke out into cries of joy. Grandpa screamed, too. He was so excited that he completely forgot about his former life, he even forgot about his own baby son. He never saw him go to school and grow up. He never heard him cry in the night, but that he didn't tell me. I guessed it.

We sat in a clearing of the thicket I'd discovered long ago and would return to whenever I had an opportunity. From time to time, a rowboat with a couple in it passed by, and I described it to Grandpa in detail, and thought to myself that maybe once Nimrod would invite me to go rowing. The man stopped rowing and gave the oars to the woman, and when he saw me watching, he waved at me. "They reversed roles," said Grandpa. "If he should fall asleep, she'll row right into the heart of the sea."

"I hope they don't drown."

"If the woman holds onto the oars, they won't drown."

The tangle of bulrushes was lovely. We could hide there for hours. Anybody strolling by paid no attention to us. Grandpa pulled up some blades of grass and stuck them between his teeth. I told him that, in the rainy season, the Yarkon is covered in wood sorrel, and that we chew on the juicy stalks, which shocks Mother, as usual: "Have you gone crazy? You can't eat like that from a field. Who knows if some dog hasn't made peepee on it!"

We sat until the light softened and a slight breeze began to ruffle the foliage. I forgot that he was my grandfather. He was like a regular friend. I was glad that Daddy had found him in America. Even if he had brought back the wrong grandfather—for after thirty-five years, a mistake like that was quite possible—I didn't care. As far as I was concerned, he could have been a total stranger. The main thing was that he was himself.

I didn't ask him about the boy in the closet or about Granny's dress.

As I helped him up the stairs, we heard footsteps padding behind us. I knew immediately who was tapping me on the shoulder.

"Grandpa, meet Nimrod. He lives on the second floor. He helps me tend the flowerpot."

They shook hands like grown-ups. Nimrod examined him with curiosity. Grandpa's eyes were clear. It was hard to tell he was blind. Nimrod didn't back off from him. He treated him like a normal person.

"There's just me and my father, that's all," said Nimrod.

"Someday you'll get married and have a lot of children."

Nimrod opened the door to his flat. "That's no substitute."

We climbed another floor. I angled the key and heard Nimrod close his door gently. Grandpa hesitated and didn't enter. When he spoke, the echo of his voice resounded in the stairwell.

"You know how I can picture your father as a small

boy? How he attended school, how he grew up?"

"You told me that you need a bunch of imagination in the cor-ri-dor."

"Through you, I see everything. Just by seeing you."

But I didn't ask how he could see without eyes. He touched one of my braids, and then we went inside.

13

"She's going to her grandfather again?"

"Are you kidding? *Not* to that old blind man! She's going there for that boy Nimrod!"

They were working in their garden. Avigdor was raking up the grass and Hemda was clipping chrysanthemums with huge shears. An enormous pile already lay beside her. She had practically cleaned out the entire garden. Only at the edges, a few flowers were left.

Hemda giggled. "What are you running after him for? He can escape from you. He has a bicycle. . . ."

"Boys don't like girls chasing them," said Avigdor, leaning on the rake, "and besides, you're a baby to him, Gershona Primadonna."

The horse stabled inside me began kicking.

"You're just jealous," I said. "And all you do is echo her like a parrot. Can't you think for yourself?"

"Why are you all hot and bothered?" said Avigdor, feigning interest. "Someone might think . . ."

"She's all excited because she's in love with him. Right, Gershona? So you found a boy with a bike."

"He's no boy," I said.

"You really think he cares about you? Do you realize he's already gone? A van came by and took him and his father. They had a big trunk. Did he say good-bye to you at least?"

I froze.

"How do you know?"

"We saw," Avigdor informed me with a look of victory on his face. "See, we're right! He didn't even tell you! Some friend!"

I fled. I didn't want to hear another word from them. I ran across the mounds of sand to the end of the block. My skirt got white from the dust. I climbed to the second floor and banged on the door. Nobody answered. I looked around but found no note. I went up to the roof and suddenly saw that the flowerpot was missing. The brick stood orphaned. The little awning still offered shade, and the wall that once protected the pot from the Cohen family's cat no longer had anything to protect. Again I went to the second floor and stormed the door.

"Nimrod!" I shouted. "Nimrod! Open up! It's me, Gershona!" I even said my name, because I had no choice.

The door stood before me, hard and punishing. The staircase shook from my stomping feet, and the echo rang from top to bottom. The next-door neighboor shot out from her apartment, furious. Her hair was set in rollers. Old witch, we called her behind her back.

"What are you yelling about? It's afternoon now. They left, they're gone! Now you get out of here, too. It's supposed to be quiet here from two to four!"

I didn't go up to my grandparents' apartment. I didn't even remove my knapsack, which rode my back and rocked with each step. I ran downstairs, and each stair felt like a block of cement. At the bottom, the mailman stood, calmly portioning out the letters. When he saw me, his face lit up. "So you live *here,* then," he said. "Show me where to put the mail for Janek Orlovski. Another letter came for him from Poland, and this is the correct address."

"There's no Janek here! Don't you understand Hebrew? I already told you so. Don't go looking for Poles in this building. There is only one new immigrant here and he's from America, and his name isn't Orlovski. Nobody even knows his name. People can hide their names if they want to. They can even hide themselves, and that's all there is to it. You hear? There is no Janek here!"

I wiped my nose on the sleeve of my blouse. It was lucky Granny didn't see that. But I really wanted to be a "barbarian." I left the mailman and ran like the wind, until I reached the Yarkon and dropped into the thicket. Into the little crater I called "my nook." My face was smothered in the ground and my body ached all over. The enchanted seed inside me exploded, and the bits and pieces cut into me everywhere. I was still attached to the knapsack. I hadn't the strength to remove it. I lay all coiled up among the thick plants. The shards of that seed shifted from one place to another, lacerating me. At first, they streaked through me, then slowed some, and finally settled down in various locations, quietly aching and murmuring like cats. I listened as that purring of theirs escaped from my throat, which was stuffed with tall grass. Then I didn't hear a thing. I entered Grandpa's corridor and fell asleep.

I dreamed that Mother's hand was caressing me. Her fingertips hovered gently over me. She had lovely hands. Starkman said that when she serves fifty grams of yellow cheese to a customer with that delightful hand of hers, the customer has no choice but to make a purchase. She told me once, blushing, that a customer asked her if he could also buy her hand.

I whispered, "Mother, is it already morning? I want to sleep some more. It's so early. Just another drop." But Mother didn't answer. It seemed to me as though she removed my blanket, because suddenly I had the chills. When I opened my eyes, I saw nobody's hand. I discovered that I wasn't even in bed. The fat leaves of some plant were nodding up and down and caressing my cheek. The sun wasn't blinding anymore, and the Yarkon was drifting past me in the direction of Reading Beach. I didn't understand what I was doing there.

Suddenly I heard her screaming. Her voice frightened me. It was drenched in grief. "Gershona! Gershona!"

I lifted myself on my elbows, but the knapsack dragged me back down. Her voice came toward me like a shaky ladder.

I tried to scream, "I'm here!" But it emerged more like a whisper.

She ran through the high grass, knocking against stones and the dry branches fallen from the eucalyptus trees, then dropped beside me, taking me in her two arms and rocking me back and forth. Her tears were streaming down her neck, and the entire front of her dress was soaking wet. I didn't believe that it was my mother. After all, I thought she never cried.

"What have you done? What have you done to me?" she wailed.

"I just . . ."

I was unable to fill in the rest and she slapped my face hard. The sound of that smack made the grass jump. It cut through the stillness. The pain was awful, the shame . . .

She broke into more sobs. "We've been looking for you for hours. The worry was driving me crazy. I thought I lost you. *They* couldn't kill me but *you* can! What are you doing to me? How could you disappear like that, without saying a word? Don't you understand what it does to me?"

She kept repeating the word "God," as if she wanted to tell Him something.

My tongue felt heavy. I wanted to get angry over the slap, I wanted to scream back at her, but my throat gagged too much.

"If anything happens to you, I wouldn't survive! Never do anything like this again, because I don't know what would happen to me. Have pity on me, pity."

She really scared me. I'd never heard her talk like this before. She suddenly looked like a little girl, with her face covered in her hands and the tears slipping between her fingers. I didn't know what to do. My anger transformed into a huge pain. Then she embraced me again with all her might, circling my whole head and drawing it against hers. The wetness transferred to me by way of my hair; she felt how my body was trying to free itself. But she wouldn't let go. I felt strangled.

"Forgive me, my child. Forgive me, Gershona."

As soon as she said "forgive me," I cried along with her, and when she said "Gershona," my mouth began howling sobs as loud as hers. The name didn't sound so ugly.

"Forgive me," she said. I didn't know parents had to ask forgiveness of a child. It's not right; it's not fair. They're the ones who know everything. A child is ignorant. They teach her everything, except what they keep secret.

"Mother, Mother, why didn't you invite me to the wedding?"

Her sobs stopped instantly. All her tears dried up in a second. Now I saw how pale she could get. I felt as if I had slapped her and not the other way around. She let go of me, and I fell backward.

"You *know!* How do you know about it?"

I didn't answer her.

She came closer and tried to force me to do the same, but I squirmed loose.

"How could we tell you?"

She sat me down gently and then slowly undid the straps of my knapsack from my shoulders. The whole time, I was lugging it on my back. I didn't even feel how heavy it was, until its weight was gone.

"It's such a sad story," she said, "and I have no explanations. An adult will understand no more of it than what a child could. It deals with questions that have no answers whatsoever. Your father has been asking them all his life. He thought that when he finally met his father, he would solve some of the riddles, but he was disappointed. Even Grandfather couldn't help him. He tried but failed. All these years, he couldn't come up with the answers himself. Maybe he didn't even dare to ask such questions. I accompanied your father to the port, and he sailed to America to meet a father he had never seen before, a father who had abandoned him when he was six months old, never to return. Your father asked me, 'How will I recognize him? After all, I never saw him my whole life!' Your father despaired, and it's just make-believe that a father and son can sense each other without any constraints of time or space."

"So how did he know that he was the one?" I stretched my hand out to her, and she trembled, perhaps on account of the chill in the air.

"Daddy hung a sign on his chest with his name on it. It was awful. I wasn't there, but I can't stop thinking about it. The ship approached New York Harbor. There were hordes of people there, and they hugged and kissed one another on the dock, falling on each other's necks. Your father leaned against the boat railing. His whole body was bent over it. And he saw an old man standing on the shore. And the old man had a sign with his name on it, attached by a safety pin to his shirt pocket. A gruesomely simple way for a father and son to identify one another. They hadn't even planned it that way."

My love for her was so great now, and I no longer attached any importance to my humiliation, or even to that slap, although it was the first time she had raised her hand to me. Her long dark hair, which she always wore gathered at her neck, came loose. She looked to me like a young girl. She reminded me of the boy in the photograph. And when she had talked about my father, I realized that she was the one who gave him all the hugs that were missing from his life.

Then we went home.

14

That night, I dreamed I was climbing upstairs to a roof. And despite the dark all around me, I was not afraid. I told myself in the dream that Grandpa, too, had learned how not to be frightened of the darkness in his corridor. The Cohen family's cat, which now I knew was called Mitzi, was roaming the wall. But he didn't jump around. He was a very serious cat now. His back was arched, and his eyes sparkled in the dark as he gazed at me without even yowling.

"Mitzi," I said, "maybe you know where the flowerpot is? Maybe you know what happened to my radishes? Maybe you can tell me where Nimrod went? And why he left?" And why, and why, and why . . .

Mitzi kept looking at me, and I was sure he understood. If not all my questions, at least one of them. He could choose which one he wanted to answer. As he swished his tail, I felt miserable over not understanding cats. Even in my dreams, the only language I knew was Hebrew and a little Yiddish. And cats never speak Yiddish in anybody's dreams.

I didn't dare peer over the small wall, since I already knew that the flowerpot was gone, and that I would never grow anything again, as I had vowed to myself. Mitzi suddenly meowed, but her meow sounded like the wail of a baby, and all at once, I heard my mother's voice reaching me from some far-off place, "Pity me, have pity."

I woke up. It's not clear to me how it works, but when I'm stuck in a nightmare, I give myself the command to immediately wake up. But right away the question appears—like on a blackboard—what if it's not a dream? It's still not clear to me if there's any danger that bad dreams could ever come true. Daddy says, "Nonsense"— a dream is just the extra stuff in life we never got around to having or doing. It's not good or bad, it's just another installment, tacked on—the more amazing or strange, the better. All extras are like that, he says.

I thought of my mother in the next room, behind the closed door. She thought I hadn't noticed, but I knew that she took a sleeping pill to help her fall asleep. The white pills were wrapped in white paper and rested beside her bed, and I was always afraid that she would get groggy and swallow all of them at one time.

I hoped she wasn't dreaming about anything now. Especially not about what had occurred in the afternoon. The wail of a cat climbed into the house and then vanished. I thought about Grandpa, who lived in a house near the Yarkon, and about the vacated apartment below him. Was

Grandpa still able to dream? If a person loses his eyes, how can he see his own dreams?

One afternoon, he fell asleep in his armchair, and I went up to him. I saw every wrinkle in his face and remembered how I had touched them with my eyes shut. His tie was askew, and I straightened it for him without his knowing. For a few long minutes, I studied him, and Granny didn't enter the room. The conclusion I came to was that, when you watch somebody sleeping, it was impossible to determine by the expression on his face alone what sort of stories his head—under lock and key—was telling him. I couldn't detect any changes in his behavior. Even his closed eyes might very well have belonged to another person. If I hadn't known that he was blind, I never would have guessed it. Someday I'll have the guts to ask him about his dreams. Whether they're blurry or dark, or like what you see through sunglasses. Or maybe in a blind man's eyes, everything looked altogether different. What did I look like to him in a dream, not as I was? Did I become different? If Daddy was right, then I was something extra, what never happened to him in real life. Not good, not bad, just another version.

The house wasn't totally still. I tucked my blanket up to my chin and listened to the *tick-tock* of the kitchen clock, the one that I wouldn't let them put in my room. Its constant beat makes my face twitch, and then I realize that my heart is beating all the time without my even noticing. Tonight the clock didn't bother me. The cat resumed wailing. I knew it couldn't be Mitzi, because the house at the end of the block was too far away. I searched for the seed inside me. The pain was gone. The broken pieces had stopped moving around, they had decomposed and seen their last days. Once we got back—Mother and I—nobody mentioned what had happened. I listened carefully before I fell asleep, but they weren't speaking in any foreign language or even whispering.

I tried to comfort myself and understand Nimrod. Maybe it was just hard to part from somebody you cared about. Maybe even Grandpa didn't say good-bye to Granny when he left her. The bits inside me weren't convinced, and what pained me the most was the thought that I might never see Nimrod again. That unique gesture of his, his hand on his blond hair. He probably won't lose that habit even when he grows up. That's how I'll be able to identify him one day on the street, and he won't be a total stranger to me. And when he has a car, he'll drive it forward a bit, then backward a bit. But if people don't change when they grow up, how come Grandpa and Daddy were unable to find in each other a single familiar detail by which to recognize each other? What did my father do with the little sign he hung from his neck? Dad must have worked hard on the lettering. Did he write it in English or Hebrew? He always told me that when he lived in Europe, before the war, he constantly practiced his Hebrew, so that one day when he reached Israel, he would be able to read and write immediately. Mother also wrote in a beautiful script when she lived in Europe before the war, much better than mine: she intended to go shopping in Israel with a list ready at hand. But I don't think she guessed then that she would herself be working in a grocery in Israel. At that time, she probably still hoped to be somebody altogether different.

A caravan of thoughts travel through me at night. Without any traffic signs, "Go slow," "Stop," "Caution." They learned from Nimrod's bicycle how to proceed a bit forward and a little backward. His wheels began swirling before my eyes, likewise the groove in the sand. Finally I fell asleep.

Daddy woke me, and that came as a real surprise. He erased all the tail ends of my dream, sat on the bed, and hugged me.

"Don't you have to go to work?" I asked drowsily. "Aren't they expecting you at the office?"

"Not today. I notified them I'd be late. That maybe I wouldn't show up at all."

"They'll be angry at you if you suddenly vanish."

"I don't know how to disappear."

"For example, travel to another country."

He pulled the blanket over me, and my feet peeked out at the other end.

"But he finally came back," said Daddy, though his voice lacked all joy.

I stuck my head out from the blanket. "Have you forgiven him for abandoning you?"

"Do you forgive me?"

"For what?" I asked, surprised.

"For creating you."

I breathed deeply, thinking that nobody chose to be born, but I didn't say so. I knew that it would hurt his feelings.

My feet peeked out from the blanket. I wiggled my big toe. "Did you know that you're older than the State of Israel?"

"But she has much longer legs than I do." And I wiggled all my toes.

"This is the second time that my parents asked me to forgive them . . ." I began to say, but stopped myself. What was happening to them? Everything was topsy-turvy. Maybe I was mother and father—and they were children? Look how Daddy was trying to get out of going to work and was just waiting for me to become angry at him and urge him to get moving. Soon they would change the name of his firm to "Shirkers Ltd."

"What does one do when one stays home?" asked Daddy.

"Play games, read a book, watch people on the street."

"You like to observe people?"

"They never even notice. I just don't like when they look back at me."

Daddy said, "Your feet will get cold," and he battled with the blanket.

"Why are you both such worriers?"

He leaned on his elbow. "When you grow up," he said, "you'll actually want others to look at you."

"How do you know what'll happen to me? You're only a father, not a prophet."

He hugged me again, and his arms were like a second blanket. His wedding ring, though, was cold.

"You're right," he said. "A father isn't such a big deal."

He pulled up the edge of the blanket and said, "You've grown a lot lately, my God! In a few months, you'll be Bat Mitzvah. Afterward you're going to grow and grow, and I won't even notice it, but you'll suddenly turn into a woman."

I grinned. "A woman? Really, Daddy!" My chest was flat as a board, only my hips had rounded a bit.

"Soon quite a few nice things will be happening to you," said Daddy.

"Just don't ever say, 'When I was your age.' I hate when people tell me that."

"I'll never say it."

"You'll forget."

Daddy pinched me. "You'll forget, too. One day you'll tell it to your own children. You'll long for something, but you won't be able to say what you're longing for."

"A pillow fight," I said, "that's what I'm longing for."

"Onward!" shouted Daddy and yanked the pillow from under my head.

I ran to the other room and brought back another pillow. I climbed into bed again as he tossed the pillow at me and missed. I tossed mine at him and it caught him smack in the face.

"It doesn't hurt at all," shouted Daddy. "Don't worry!"

I wasn't worried. The pillows went flying and not a feather broke loose. How we laughed! Daddy laughed so hard that tears began rolling down his cheeks.

"Do you know that he plucked chickens when he first came to America? Maybe these pillows are stuffed with his feathers."

Daddy placed the pillow on the bed and straightened it. "I didn't know how exhausting a pillow fight could be," he said. "You have to go to school now."

"It's the end of the year. We don't learn anything important now," I said, getting up anyway.

Daddy stroked my head. "Sometimes I think you already know everything."

He stretched out on the bed, and I didn't disturb him. He folded his arms under his head and lay there quietly. I stole a glance at the knapsack resting beside the door.

"Do you think Mother will be angry?"

"She told me that she hit you."

I lowered my head. "She didn't mean to. . . ." My cheek, as I touched it, was ice-cold.

"Nobody hit me," whispered Daddy and closed his eyes. I waited. He was breathing deeply.

"Are you asleep, Daddy?"

He opened his eyes and looked up at the white ceiling. "I must tell you something about 'when I was your age.' Don't get angry. It's the last time. Back then . . . I wanted so badly to have a father."

I grabbed my clothes and went to another room to get dressed. Daddy didn't say another word. When I returned, he folded my pajamas and pulled the blanket exactly up to the pillow, which now sagged where his head had lain. He looked at me as I loaded the knapsack on my back.

"You're not going to work?" I asked.

"Your knapsack is crooked," he said. "I'll stay a bit longer. It's really nice at home in the morning. Even the Plymouth is glad to have a day off. Why not, doesn't she deserve it?"

I opened the door and saw it. My flowerpot. It stood there proud and in bloom. Each flower spread a cluster of petals of a different color. Violet and orange and red and yellow all leaped out at my eyes.

"Daddy! Daddy! Come quickly!" I was so excited.

Both of us stared at that wondrous pot of flowers. The fragrance spread throughout the stairwell.

"How did it get here? How did it grow so fast?"

I raised the pot, and the flowers didn't resemble radish blossoms. But that didn't offend me in the least. I caressed them. And something dropped. It wasn't a leaf. Just a tiny note with three words on it. "From me, Nimrod."

15

Intense joy is hard to describe. Pain is easy. When I pity myself—and I was doing a lot of that lately—it feels good at first. Like being in a warm humid cave. I can sit in the midst of it and hug myself and say how miserable I am and that I'm the only one who loves me, and some day they'll bow down to me and beg me to love them for a moment.

Then the cave gets sticky and uncomfortable and all my previous pleasure evaporates. So maybe pitying myself isn't the best answer. Perhaps laughing at myself would be better.

This joy of mine wasn't like any surprise gift. Nor was it like the new shoes I got every year for Passover. It was just seeing the flowerpot alive, with its multicolored crowns and perfumed fragrance that penetrated under my skin.

He didn't forget me. He went away, but he came back.

Hemda called out to me from downstairs, asking why I hadn't come to class and if I wanted the homework. I yelled down to her, "Liar!" and slammed the window shut, despite the heat.

My whole body wanted to sing, not just my mouth, even my toes—even the fingernail of my pinky. The broken slivers inside me vanished all at once, out they went and without a single lesion. All day I was drawn to that flowerpot and gently petted its leaves. By evening they folded to sleep. I'll never forget this day—the pillow fight in the morning and the afternoon trip we took together in the Plymouth. We drove almost to the highway heading for Jerusalem, and I waved out the window to every passing car. Then we drove to the grocery to pick Mother up. We saved her the walk home in the heat. She, too, got caught up in my joy, and I think she forgot for a moment what had happened yesterday and those two white sleeping pills of hers by her bedside. Starkman couldn't figure out what was going on and asked if there was any news about Grandfather's eyes. Daddy shook his head from side to side, and Starkman looked disappointed, but decided to give me a free popsicle.

The shutters in Nimrod's apartment were closed. Maybe he'd returned for two minutes in order to place the pot by my door, and immediately afterward traveled to some mysterious place of his. When I went upstairs, nobody answered. The neighbor opened her door and peeked. "I hope you're not going to start up your commotion again. It's supposed to be quiet here between two and four." And she slammed her door.

An envelope was stuck under Nimrod's door. I was very

curious and did something improper. Carefully drawing it out, I peeked at what was written on it. The letter was addressed to Janek Orlovski. That *nudnik* of a mailman doesn't give up, I thought to myself. What a good-for-nothing. I'd told him straight out that there was no such person here. And that he should look elsewhere. So why did he shove the letter into Nimrod's apartment, of all places? Neither Nimrod nor his father had time to go searching for a man from Poland who got too much mail.

This Janek business, though, didn't detain me for long, since I was still involved in my own happiness, celebrating it in my cave with images of Nimrod growing up and of the two of us riding our bikes along the length of the Yarkon—to the seventh ferry stop—while Hemda was bursting with envy. In the cave of self-pity, such are the biggest pleasures. Her garden full of flowers wasn't as lovely as my little flowerpot. My magic radishes. The gardener won't believe his eyes.

Toward evening, I went back there again. This time I had to get my grandpa into my joy.

"I told you that the whole secret was sunshine." He smiled in victory. "I knew it would vanquish your friends. You simply have to know how to ask it for help. There is something good about this land—the sun is very close by. Whereas if you climb all the way to the top of the Empire State building, you wouldn't be as close. That's the way it goes, it doesn't depend on height."

Daddy opened the door and offered Grandpa a glass of tea. I was sure that he had heard Grandpa's explanation. He mumbled, "Well, well"—that's what he always mumbled when he was in a daze. He wanted to read the New

York Stock Exchange numbers in my stead, and I listened to the way he pronounced those bizarre words. His voice got soft and low, and now and again he stopped to rest. The newspaper concealed his face, and I remembered our morning conversation and was glad for him that he found a father. It may not be such a big deal, but it's something.

Every two minutes or so, Granny came in and went out. She acted like a guard. As if she feared that any moment a quarrel would break out between them and she would have to make peace. Grandpa asked Daddy for the newspaper and folded it into a narrow strip, crowded with letters. Daddy asked him why he was saving it, and he answered that it was a special paper. I didn't understand why. It seemed to me that I was reading the same thing every day. I didn't ask them. I saw that they were sad.

I decided to say good-bye to the roof. After all, the roof had helped the pot to flower. Some tenant was busy in the laundry room. I saw the steam rising slowly above the awning. If I hadn't known it was a house, I might have thought for a minute that I was on a ship.

I surveyed the surroundings. The Tel Aviv rooftops were bright, and the houses themselves looked like gray dice. Even the sea was visible from a corner of the roof, if I stood on my tiptoes.

Now I was the tallest person in the city. I could see all the sandlots. Nobody was on the scaffolds, since the workers had already gone home. I approached the little wall and got down on all fours. I pretended that I was a spy and had a scheme up my sleeve. I had to notify my superiors about what was going on in my secret sector.

But a surprise was waiting for me there. The flowerpot

stood in its usual spot. Just as if it hadn't disappeared yesterday.

At first I thought I was imagining it, but I quickly understood the truth. The pot with all the flowers was not the pot that I had tended to all these months. What a disappointment! I wanted to abandon it, to toss it over the roof into the wind. The secret was not in the sun; Grandpa was mistaken. That wasn't the first time he was in error. I wanted to kick that awful pot, which swallowed seeds and didn't prove a darn thing.

Before I could raise my foot against it, my eye caught something green moving there. That was impossible, I told myself, you're just imagining again. Nonetheless, I came closer to it— what could I lose?

The circle of soil was covered in tiny leaves. Like weak puppies, a few hours old. It really was fatiguing to grow at long last. At the bottom of the pot a crack showed. Maybe the result of Mitzi's prowling in the night.

The clamor in the laundry room ended. The tenant stepped out, and the metal washtub piled high with wet clothing completely concealed her.

I said, "It's just me, the grandchild of your neighbor on the third floor."

The washtub shifted, and behind it stood Nimrod. His blond hair was damp and his cheeks flushed. He set the tub down and took a break from his labor.

"You came back!" I screamed, and immediately felt ashamed. Hemda had declaimed in class that it was a great disgrace for a girl to chase after boys. It was forbidden to show them your real feelings—that was the rule. Lately she gave advice to all the girls, considering herself an expert, though on what basis I had no idea. Maybe because her mother read romantic novels in German like my granny.

We sat by the little wall. Nimrod toyed with the bricks and managed to pull out two of them. The gap widened. The wall was on the verge of collapsing. "We don't need it anymore," he said.

"The flowers are splendid," I said, "you ought to come see them."

"If I knew that these leaves would sprout overnight . . ."

"You wouldn't have delivered the other pot to me?"

"I know nothing about flowers. What kind of flowers are growing in this pot? The leaves look strange."

"What's the difference?" I said. "I'll be happy with anything that comes up."

Then we grabbed the two handles of the washtub, which we called a "bowl," and we started hanging the wet laundry. We removed his father's blue work pants and khaki shirts. It was a mountain of men's clothing without a single nightgown or slip.

"I brought you the flowerpot from the kibbutz. That's where I went with my father."

"They told me you left."

"Is that the way people leave?" he asked, surprised, and stretched the sleeve of a shirt.

"I don't know. That's just what I thought."

He handed me another sleeve and I fastened it with a clothespin.

"Actually, there are some people who do take off like that," said Nimrod, "and you should know that it's not always your fault. Suddenly something occurs and they have to flee, and there just isn't time to say good-bye."

"Anybody who is left like that never forgets it," I said. "Like my dad."

Nimrod handed me the cuff of a blue trouser leg. We turned it the other way to reach the line. "If we ever don't have a chance to say good-bye, we can always reach each other with our minds. Anything can be accomplished with the mind, you understand?"

I kept quiet. The pants got tangled in the rope, and I wasn't able to unravel them.

"You don't get it. How could you? You've always lived here. You were born here, right?"

"And *you* weren't?"

Something murky hung in the air. A gust of wind erupted at the far end of the roof and rocked the heavy clotheslines. The wash started swaying and covered him up. "Nimrod," I shouted, "where are you?"

For a moment, it seemed as though he had vanished. The big sheet we had hung with such effort had struck him and swaddled him whole. I broke out laughing. I told him that the ancient Greeks looked like that. We began playing hide-and-seek among the wash, and afterward we raced the length of the roof. We played until the sun disappeared behind the last houses.

"One day Tel Aviv will reach that far!" Nimrod pointed in the direction of the hills on the horizon.

"You're wrong," I said. "Nobody will dare to build a housing project on Anemone Hill. Otherwise there'll be nowhere to go on Saturday. And besides, how many people do you think will ever reach here?"

The sound of footsteps came from the doorway to the staircase.

"Somebody's on the way up here," I said, a little embarrassed. "Maybe another tenant remembered he had some dirty laundry."

First the hand showed, groping along the wall, then out stepped Grandpa. He walked upright, holding onto the walls.

"Children," he said, "you have forgotten yourselves. It's late."

He wasn't angry at us. If there was any anger in him, he knew how to conceal it from me.

We followed him through the dark passageway. He went first, Nimrod next, and I hung back for another second. The ropes bowed under their load of laundry. As I passed by I pinched the big sheet, and it was already almost dry.

16

On the following day, I came of age. And not by my own decision. My parents held a secret convocation, concluding that I had turned into, if not a full-fledged adult, then at least a half-fledged one.

They informed me that from today on, I would have my own key, and I could come and go as I pleased. I was a free girl, they said, as though they had earlier considered me a prisoner. Except, of course, that I'd always have to notify them exactly where I was going and when I'd be back.

Mother couldn't help but add, "And you should know that in case of an emergency, Starkman will let you call from the grocery, if Simha isn't home or her telephone happens to be on the blink. I'm not sure if you know Daddy's number at work by heart."

Naturally I knew it, and naturally I recited it for her

twenty times over. She used to test me now and then—practice for that emergency of hers. My mother persisted in anticipating dangers. I'm positive that if she were asked about it, she would say in all seriousness that "it wasn't altogether impossible for a leopard to be lurking somewhere in the thickets along the Yarkon."

I truly admired her courage in this matter of the key. I don't think that Daddy influenced her. She wove a thick braid from nylon gimp, so that I should have my own key holder, which was a real sign that she had given it much thought and had meant every word she said, even though it was difficult for her.

She handed it to me all wrapped up, tied with a string as if it were some ceremony, accompanied with instructions. "Wear it around your neck," she recommended.

"Are you kidding?" I said. "They'll think I'm a cow!"

"Okay, then pick some fixed place in your knapsack so you won't forget it. And the main thing is not to lose it, otherwise it'll be very unpleasant."

Behind those words "very unpleasant" could lurk all sorts of disasters—from burglary to war. Each and every "God forbid" and "We should never know of it."

Daddy tapped her shoulder. "All right, enough instructions. She could recite them all in the middle of the night, I'm sure. We agreed that she was an adolescent now."

Mother was a little embarrassed. "It's not so simple," she said, still holding onto the key. "If we had other children . . ."

That's how the key became my present for the summer vacation.

The true test for Mother was the ferry line that opened

on the Yarkon to Reading Beach. She hesitated before she'd permit me to board a ferry unaccompanied by an adult. I convinced her that I would never go by myself.

Already on the first day of the vacation, Hemda came upstairs to ask if I wanted to join her and a few other friends. "Avigdor won't be there," she emphasized. I really didn't like him. I suspected that my mother had spoken with her mother, requesting that I be invited, but I had no proof. I decided not even to worry about it. I wanted very badly to go on a rowboat. I remembered the couple who went rowing past me and Grandpa on the Yarkon.

She waited for me to put on my bathing suit, and as we went down the steps, she asked, "What about Nimrod? Maybe we should invite him, too?" She lowered her head, and then looked in another direction.

On the ferry, nobody called me "Gershona Primadonna." I had a key now. I had even grown two full centimeters, and my chest was beginning to ache.

A few days later, Avigdor came along, too. I didn't exchange a single word with him. I kept looking at the far side of the ferry. But he said nothing and didn't bring up the subject of the garden. I sensed his eyes hanging on me, tracking me even when we came ashore. I asked myself what he was scheming. After days of this, I began feeling that his gaze was actually pleasant, like a longing of sorts. He instilled in me the hope that I would one day see a similar look of longing in somebody's eyes—but certainly not his.

At first I was careful to hang the key around my wrist, like a bracelet. But the heat was unbearable and, also, I was afraid that the waves would undo the knot and sweep the key into the sea. That was all I needed. I got into the habit of leaving it in my straw basket. I could pick it out of there easily by the multicolored nylon braid. A dog came by once and knocked over the basket. All my belongings spilled onto the sand. Before I had a chance to gather everything up, Avigdor handed me the key.

"If you ever lose it, you can come over to us."

I said thank you and turned my back on him. I was confused. What sort of a prank was he concocting now in that nasty head of his?

I was assigned a new responsibility for the afternoon. I would lead Grandpa on his daily stroll. Granny had complained that, during the torrid hours of the morning, it took too much out of her. Grandpa waited patiently until I arrived. And Nimrod would come along with us, too.

My hand would be placed in Grandpa's big palm, as Nimrod rode his bike alongside us. When he would get ahead of us, he would say that he was the cyclist who was blazing the trail for the king.

"Grandpa"—he got accustomed to calling him Grandpa—"is there a king in America?"

"No, no, just a president. Like here. They elect somebody who has accomplished something important, like General Eisenhower, who defeated the Nazis."

"Too bad we don't have a king," I said.

"In all of Tel Aviv, there isn't a single house that looks like a castle," said Nimrod. "No king would agree to live in a housing project. Kings have certain requirements."

"And what about ordinary people?" insisted Grandpa.

Nimrod laughed. "They want to live in a palace, too, but they know that it's a hopeless dream."

"So what's their dream, then?" asked Grandpa.

"Just to live," said Nimrod, and pedalled away fast. He was far off before he made a big turn and came back.

Grandpa never took off his suit jacket or his tie. He was always dressed handsomely. Pedestrians stared at him, not because he was blind but, in my opinion, because he was the most elegant old man in Tel Aviv.

He chose a new tie every day, he never wore the same tie twice in a row. He had a gigantic collection on his closet door. In spite of the heat, not a single drop of sweat ever ran down his forehead. Our clothes stuck to us, while he remained fresh, as though the sun didn't dare get close to him. I finally decided that even if they had brought the wrong grandfather by mistake, they had found a suitable match for Granny anyway.

"Granny says you look like a street urchin. That you don't have even one proper dress."

I denied it. I said I had a skirt that folded like a fan, and Grandpa promised that for my Bat Mitzvah they would buy me a genuine dress. Maybe he thought that the bridal shop on Allenby Street also had dresses for adolescent girls.

Nimrod said that on Friday nights and on holidays, he wore blue pants and a white shirt. I remembered how we had hung them on the line to dry, and I thought to myself how delighted I would be to see him once in holiday gear. And when school starts again, I'll invite him to a Friday evening celebration in our class when we dance in couples. Then we'll see if Hemda has the nerve to approach him.

We never saw his father at all. Come six o'clock, Nimrod would look at his watch—he was the only boy I knew who had one—and say that he had to go upstairs and wait for his father. He said he had to prepare supper for him. He still hadn't invited me to visit his home.

We exchanged flowerpots. He asked if he could keep the one with the flowers at his place, and he promised to look after it faithfully. I replaced the pot of radishes on the windowsill. Each day the leaves strengthened and grew taller, and Mother said I should learn from their example.

One day, the afternoon stroll was cancelled. Grandpa complained about not feeling well, but insisted that it wasn't serious, just a common cold. I was surprised how he could catch cold in the summer, but I remembered Mother's warning never to drink ice water even in summer, because the throat is sensitive to temperature. And ice cream in winter was out of the question, since that was a real danger. Apparently Grandpa had drunk some ice water. He was unfamiliar with Mother's list of precautions.

Nimrod wasn't around then—he'd gone to the port— so I decided to go back home. I jiggled the key merrily and it climbed from my wrist to my elbow. At the entrance I bumped into the mailman. His blue mailbag was swollen with letters.

I couldn't contain myself and shouted, "Don't you have any letter today for your Janek?" Then I bolted.

"You're an insolent girl," he cried. "I'll tell your grandfather." His angry words pursued me.

I stuck the key in the slot and turned it. Every day was another contest to see if I could open the door faster than the day before.

Only after I was already inside, did I hear them. They

were whispering. But it wasn't the typical whisper of people who were telling each other secrets. In my whole life, I had never heard voices so soft.

Mother groaned. Not in pain or anguish. Her voice sounded as if she were singing. I could feel a chill crawling up my spine. Daddy's whisper was choked and tremulous. The words he spoke hit my ears clearly: "I don't want her to be an only child. Like me."

I was already next to their bedroom door. I didn't know what to do. The glass door was half open and they were reflected in it. I looked at them as if I were looking at a strange photograph. I knew they were my parents, but they didn't resemble Mother and Father. They were strewn on the bed, hugging. Apparently Starkman had sent her home early today. What happened?

The glass glittered. Daddy's face hid inside her hair, which was scattered on the pillow. As he parted her hair, he twined a strand around his finger. The sheet covered them, and only their dark heads rested above the white fabric. Their clothes lay in disarray all around them.

I felt as if a fire had broken out on my face. My legs were paralyzed. I was unable to move from the spot. I stood all shrunken, nailed to the floor. All I wanted was for them not to see me. And not to find out that I had seen them.

Never before in my life had I felt so confused, but even so, I couldn't take my eyes off the picture reflected in that glass door.

Mother's fingers were inside Daddy's curls. Her white arm wrapped around his back. I couldn't see the blue numbers. Suddenly Daddy's head rose, and he whispered,

"You're so lovely the way you are now. . . ." Mother was holding him and drawing him toward her. The sheet surged like the sea. I felt like I was drowning. The light reflected in the glass, too, and blinded me. For a moment I really couldn't see a thing.

It felt as though hours had passed. Half a lifetime. Finally my eyes sped from the soft movements in the glass. They filled with tears. I was terrified but bewitched. My parents didn't say another word; just the rustling sheet pervaded the house.

Quietly I left.

All I thought about at that moment was how to exit in silence and not bang the front door. That's how I had my first lesson in using a key while closing a door soundlessly.

17

What was I to do with so many secrets? Nobody gave them to me for safekeeping. I felt like a thief.

Was it my fault that yet another secret came to my attention? I hadn't gone looking for it. Not this time.

I wanted to yell, "It all happened by mistake," but I said nothing.

Now this secret curled up inside the earlier ones. I already had a neat pile of them at home, as if they were my winter sweaters that mother had stored away for the summer. The secrets got all jumbled and I wasn't sure anymore of what I knew; I couldn't distinguish fact from imagination. I was lost in the dark.

My confusion was so great that I even feared I might talk in my sleep and betray my parents. Why hadn't I run away from their bedroom immediately? Why had I stayed and watched in their doorway? It was impossible to erase that picture. It gave me goosebumps—that shocking yet lovely image of them in bed.

When I returned home two hours later, everything was back to normal. Without their knowing it, I searched for clues. Their bedroom was in perfect order. Clothes hanging in the closet, the bed without a wrinkle, the sheets pulled taut. Daddy was sitting on the porch on Grandpa's armchair, drinking coffee. Mother was ironing.

"Did you and Grandpa go for a walk together?" She didn't even raise her eyes from the ironing board.

"For a bit. By myself, though. Grandpa stayed home."

She shot me an inquisitive look. "You had an argument?"

"No, what for? I never argue with Grandpa."

"What's the matter with you? Don't you feel well?"

"Please, everything's fine. Really."

It amazed me that nothing in the house had changed one bit. Once again, they were my parents. I had seen Mother ironing many times, and Father sipping coffee or reading a newspaper. But now I knew that behind such simple scenes, a lot was going on.

Perhaps I appeared just as ordinary to them. They had no notion of my own secrets. I had never told them how I learned about the remarriage of Grandpa and Granny. They must have returned Granny's dress to the shop on Allenby long ago. They couldn't have realized what I went through to try to find it, and Mother didn't know that I guessed who the boy in the picture was. Some day I'll have the guts to ask her if he's really Gershon. Maybe that will happen at my Bat Mitzvah, when I'm twelve. Now, as I walked around the house, I could feel all our mysteries mingling.

Mother asked, "Are you sure you're all right? You spend too much time outdoors. I wish your vacation were over already!"

"It just began," I said softly.

"You sound like you have sunstroke. Maybe you should lie down in bed?"

Her hair was all gathered, with not a strand loose. Touching her bun, she calmed down.

"Mother . . ." I said, but didn't continue.

She lifted the iron. A brown triangular stain showed on the flattened dress, and I already knew that a stain like that wouldn't come out in the wash.

Their garden had withered. Only a few dry bristles stuck out along the edges. The rest of the flower bed was altogether bald. There wasn't a trace of all the foliage and flowers that Hemda had been so proud of. The hose lay coiled like a dead snake. Gone was the garden; it was a desert now.

"The summer was too much for it," announced Hemda. "We sure watered it enough. Maybe plants can't grow in sand. And anyway, who has patience for garden work during vacation? When school starts, we'll plant again. Don't you think we can try again?"

"Unless the soil is angry at you," I said. "It doesn't forget so quickly."

The ferryboat vibrated somewhat, and the man we called

Captain warned us not to lean over the sides. "You'd think the Yarkon River had waves," laughed Hemda.

Avigdor was quick to grab my hand, but I freed myself immediately.

"I just didn't want you to fall. That's all," he said, embarrassed.

"Big shot," teased his sister. "Dream all you wish! But you'll have to learn how to ride a bike if you want her to look at you!"

Silence fell. Avigdor rummaged nervously through his knapsack, fiddling with all his beach equipment, rearranging his set of paddles and rubber ball, fishing out his flippers and then putting them back in. He turned his back on us, looking busy.

"Aren't you ever sorry?" I asked Hemda.

She answered with a gesture that said *Of course not*, adding a moment later, "Sometime when you go out walking, you and Nimrod, I mean, invite me along, why not? I'm not just your downstairs neighbor, I'm practically your friend."

Aboard the ferry, I thought of Nimrod, and kept thinking of him all day long. Should I give him my secret? Maybe I could ask him if he thought the child in the photograph was Gershon, and if he knew of any connection between Gershon and my mother. After all, she named me after him. Maybe Nimrod had chanced on some dark secret about his father. You couldn't preserve family secrets in an album. All you could do was leaf through them before falling asleep and thereafter dream the answers.

One day the only passengers on the ferry were grown-ups. A famous Italian circus had travelled all the way from Naples to Tel Aviv, and almost every kid was downtown standing in line for tickets. Some magician was going to place a woman in a box and cut her in half. I didn't think it was something I cared to see.

There also wasn't a single kid at Starkman's Grocery when I went there shopping. The school yard was deserted too, with nobody even playing soccer. I sneaked a glance at Nimrod's blinds, but they were shut. The only friend remaining was Grandpa.

Granny opened the door, her hands dripping wet. "Come in," she said. "I'm busy still with the tub. Take a look at them swimming there." The two fish for the Sabbath meal were splashing in the bathtub.

"I don't understand how you can treat them so nicely and eat them afterward. It's cruel, I think."

Granny smiled. "What do you understand? What—is a fish human? Good gefilte fish, that's all they are. A pair of carp without a drop of fat. Didn't you study Torah? God created fish on the fifth day in order that man would have something tasty to eat the next day."

Grandpa butted in; we hadn't heard him enter the room. "Occasionally it's the other way around. Gefilte human flesh! Ever heard of such a dish?"

"You're always on her side," said Granny, leaving the kitchen, insulted.

I plunged my hand into the water but the two carp fish, superb swimmers, escaped in a flash. Not giving up, I finally managed to touch one smooth tail, while already beginning to weave a plan in my head.

After waiting a while for Granny to move farther away,

I whispered to Grandpa, "Why don't we take them back to the sea and set them free?"

His face lit up. "We must mark time until she goes out to shop. Come on, let's put them in the wash bucket."

When I returned with the pail, he said, "Not the sea. Carp live in fresh water."

"Let's try the Yarkon," I said. "It's not exactly a fresh-water river or even a river."

"Changing your mind?"

"It won't be easy to catch them," I said. Grandpa concentrated, sunk his huge hands into the water, and the two fish swam inside them as if that was their home.

The Captain looked strangely at us. Grandpa held tightly onto the bucket, and I onto him, as I helped Grandpa climb into the boat.

"No kids today?"

"They're all at the circus."

Grandpa said he could already smell the sea. He recalled the waves smacking against Ellis Island, where the immigrants all landed. He said he had never before bathed in seawater. That took me by surprise. How could anyone concern himself just with chicken feathers or the boring numbers of the Stock Exchange?

We really looked odd. Grandpa in suit and tie, his pants pressed to perfection. Suddenly, at the next stop, Avigdor got on.

Grandpa asked, "Who is that smiling at you all the time?"

"Just somebody." I was surprised he knew so many things without actually seeing them.

Avigdor craned his neck to discover what was in the

bucket, but I hid it behind my back. At the same time, I took the opportunity to cover myself so he wouldn't notice my bathing suit. Although he had already seen me at the beach, now it was different. The suit fit me like my own skin, and my chest was hurting me.

"That boy, is he the one who makes fun of you?"

"Lately he stopped bothering me. He doesn't call me Gershona Prima—please, we're getting off at this stop."

Then we saw the Yarkon merging with the sea. We both saw it, I say, since I gave Grandpa a detailed description of everything, especially the way the waves of the Mediterranean crashed into the river, trying to form one rhythm. The ferry docked. The Captain leaped to the pier and pulled on the thick rope, which was soaking wet, looping the noose around a wooden post. Avigdor hung around us.

"Need some help? How are you going to make it with your grandfather? He doesn't see anything. Your mother will be angry at you. You don't take a blind old man to the sea—and with a bucket yet! What have you got in there? I bet you've come to collect shells."

"Finished? We're getting along fine. Don't worry about us. You think a blind man can't see? Well, you should know he has his own ways."

"Okay, okay. Don't get excited. If I had a bike . . ."

We walked slowly. The grass wasn't growing anymore, probably on account of the salt. Grandpa set the bucket down and took his shoes off. A few steps more and he removed his socks.

"Why are you laughing?" he asked.

"Because you're wearing a suit and you're barefoot."

122

"That's how I can tell how close we are to water, if the soil gets soggy."

The Yarkon was rushing now, and the fish were banging in the bucket as if they could feel they were nearing their home.

"Not here," said Grandpa. "We have to go in deeper." And he removed his tie, jacket, then shirt, folding everything neatly, smoothing each item with his hand. Afterward, he slipped out of his perfectly creased pants, which were now covered in sand.

"You're wearing bathing trunks!" I cried, delighted.

"When I sent Granny out to buy them, she said I must've fallen on my head."

His body without his clothes wasn't a bit pale. Suddenly I was reminded of how he looked in that old photograph, decked in medals.

"Now give me your hand." His eyes opened wide, and he splashed himself.

"What are you feeling, Grandpa?"

"It smells of salt. This is where the Yarkon ends."

"No, that's not what I meant. Are you in love with Granny now all over again? How could you forget her for thirty-five years? Didn't you dream about her? And about your baby boy, who is now my father?"

"When I left, I didn't know I wouldn't be back. You're asking hard questions."

"I don't have any other kind."

"When a man travels to some far-off land, he packs his former life in a box and closes the lid. So it's as if the old life belonged to another person."

The bucket was heavy when we overturned it. The Yarkon swallowed the water from our tub.

"But I want to know," I said. "How will I ever know?"

The two carp flip-flopped. They had to be ecstatic about being home again. Even if the Yarkon wasn't where they had originally been caught, it would ultimately link up with the right spot, so they would finally arrive where they came from.

"In time, all things make sense. You may not know how it works, but suddenly you have a few answers. Not all of them, though."

"How does love come and go?"

"Of that, too, I have no idea. Who does? Don't think a grown-up can explain everything, particularly a blind one."

By then we were deep in water. Grandpa immersed himself without a fuss. The waves lapped against his fingers. I dove in, but even underwater, my cheeks were burning.

"How will I know if he truly loves me?"

"There are no sure signs," said Grandpa.

It felt as if Granny were with us in the water. I was sorry for her. I thought of how she must have loved him quietly, all those years. After all, she married him a second time. I wanted to ask him if he knew who the child in the photograph in the closet was, but, each time, another wave rolled over us.

Beneath the water I hugged him; despite him saying that he had never once set foot in seawater, he was a fine swimmer.

"Why does it hurt so much to learn the answers?"

Grandpa stroked my wet braid. The other braid had come apart. He muttered as if to himself, "If they ever tell me my eyes could open for no more than a blink, I'd choose to see . . . you."

The fish that we had released came into my mind. They had to be wild with joy now. Even if the Yarkon was unsuitable for carp, it was much safer than Granny's bathtub.

Once we were back on the beach, I asked, "And you wouldn't have chosen to see my father?"

Grandpa didn't reply.

18

"Something very unpleasant might have happened!"

I hid my smile.

"And I thought you were a responsible child. We decided that you were an adolescent already. You simply acted crazy. What got into you? There isn't even a lifeguard there, the way it should be!"

"There actually is!"

"And they put up a red flag. We're very disappointed in you, Gershona."

Even so, she didn't take back my key.

And this was nothing compared to the scandal at Granny's. She almost went berserk with anger, and afterward, as a sign of protest, she announced that she wouldn't be preparing any gefilte fish for at least a month. The downpour of rebukes actually amused me. No longer was

I sitting in the cave of self-pity. I'd promised myself to laugh instead.

Nimrod and I spent a marvelous hour imagining the expression on her face when she discovered that her carps had "flown the tub."

"She must have thought that she bought chickens by mistake."

I'd never seen Nimrod laugh so hard. His two rows of white teeth were arranged like Jaffa oranges in a crate. His rolling laughter was contagious. He was sorry that he had missed the fun, and the whole idea of fish in a bathtub struck him as weird.

"In our place . . ." he said, but instantly went silent.

"Yes?"

"It's not important."

"I'll never eat carp again," I said.

"Sometimes you have to wait for hours for the fish to get caught on the hook. You hold the rod still, so the fish won't suspect any hidden danger."

"Poor fish . . . he doesn't know what's awaiting him."

"Sometimes it does and still enters the trap. That's how bad it wants the bait."

"Stupid fish."

"No more stupid than people," said Nimrod, brushing his mane of hair off his forehead. "They're easy to trap, too."

"But a person wouldn't get caught by a worm," I said.

"He himself can turn into a worm. Do you know how easy it is to find worms for bait? You just dig in the ground and pull them out. They twist in their struggle to escape. Pity them, too, if you want."

I didn't tell him about my cave of misery, where I had room mainly for myself. He sank into himself as if he were dreaming about some far-off place unknown to me.

"I used to sit for hours on the pier. Gdansk has a huge wharf. The fish would come close and break away. They would check to see who was lurking there with rods and then quickly head out to sea, where they were safe."

I didn't get a chance to ask him where Gdansk was, because someone was blocking the light on the staircase. A large man in blue overalls was standing there. Nimrod shot over to him with open arms.

"Daddy!" he cried, and hugged him. "You're early! I didn't prepare supper yet!"

The man smiled at me. "So this is your charming friend who loves flowerpots?" He spoke in a foreign accent.

I blushed.

Nimrod's father extended his hand to me. We shook hands, and he apologized that his were black from working at the harbor. Then he lifted my hand to his mouth and kissed it. I blushed even more.

"You see, Nimrod, that's what a well-mannered man does."

"That's not the custom here!" Nimrod sounded disturbed.

His father answered, "This is the basic custom, important everywhere. Never forget that! Would the young lady care to join us for supper?"

I wasn't sure that Nimrod was happy with the idea. "I'll have to ask my parents."

Nimrod's father was determined. "Run home and come back quickly. We'll wait for you."

I thought to myself that he was a powerful man who could lift two crates in one hand and his son in the other.

When I returned, the door was open. On the table a white ironed tablecloth was spread. I noticed that there wasn't even a tiny wrinkle on it. I knew right away who had ironed it to such perfection. Three plates lay on the table, unlike the blue plastic ones that we ate from in our place. They were made of delicate porcelain, and in the center of each plate was the picture of a woman in a long dress and a tall hat. In the center of the table stood a candlestick with a lit candle in it, as well as a glass goblet that held a red rose. I had never seen such a lovely table in my whole life. Maybe they set tables this way at weddings, but I was never invited to the wedding, after all.

A cry of amazement slipped from my mouth. Nimrod's father moved the chair back for me. He had switched from overalls to nicer clothes, and his hair was wet from the shower.

"You're so quick," I said.

"Nimrod's faster than I. You still don't know all his gifts. Do you realize how fast he can climb stairs? A real cat. Even a spiral staircase in a narrow tower. One minute he's here, and the next he's gone, as if the earth had swallowed him. Nobody can catch him!"

"Father!" protested Nimrod. His voice sounded angry the whole time. He went to the kitchen and brought back some white cheese and a bowl of olives. I wanted to help him, but Nimrod's father stopped me.

"We go by the rules of etiquette."

"I don't know them so well." I thought he would find

favor in Granny's eyes, since he was the opposite of a barbarian.

Nimrod went back to the kitchen and returned with some slices of bread that were extremely thick. His father looked with amazement at them, but said nothing.

All evening, he called me "young lady," and never once asked my name. I wouldn't have minded it by now if he had asked. I'll never change my name anyway. But apparently names weren't so important to him. Secretly I looked around. The house was almost empty and the rooms bare. Just two iron beds were there, with gray woolen blankets on them, and they were side by side along the length of the wall. The walls were glossy, as if they'd been whitewashed recently. Above one of the beds a picture hung, but I couldn't make out the details from afar, and the light didn't penetrate there either.

"We didn't bring anything with us," said Nimrod's father when he noticed me looking around. "We left everything behind. It's a pity. We had to leave even Nimrod's fishing rod and binoculars there."

Nimrod said very little. He let his father do all the talking for him. It pained me to see him so perplexed. I didn't understand why he was so ashamed. His father seemed charming to me.

Even the way he drew out his words, one by one.

"But in the desert, you don't need a fishing pole," said Nimrod's father. "There's nothing to fish for. The binoculars, though, would have come in handy, to locate some water."

"The desert?" I asked.

"Didn't Nimrod tell you? We're going down to the

Negev to settle there. A kibbutz is like a boat, except it doesn't toss in the night during a storm."

"You're really leaving?" My voice grew fainter.

"Didn't he tell you? Very strange. We travelled there for a visit recently. Houses will be built there. For now there are cabins, and no trees at all. Finding shade will be a problem. But one day, the place will be a paradise, you'll see. Will you come visit us?"

"I don't know." Suddenly I wanted to go home. The shards of the seeds awoke inside me and began moaning.

Nimrod said, "Wait a bit, don't go."

I helped clear the table. I was afraid to stack the dishes in a pile, so I took each one separately. The glorious woman smiled at me from the depths of the plate, and her dress, which was covered in white cheese, looked like a wedding gown.

"This plate has a crack," I said.

"You can hardly see it," said Nimrod and set it in the sink, gingerly. He turned on the faucet but didn't do any washing; he just looked at me.

Nimrod's father called out from the other room, "Another letter came! She doesn't forget you."

Nimrod turned colors and shoved all the dishes under the faucet. The water streamed over them and splashed me, too. The seed's splinters began shifting in place. Now I knew that everybody has secrets and hides them especially from anyone he holds dear. I didn't ask who the person sending him the letters was, but I knew that she was right to remember him. There was nothing he could do about that. He said that, in his family, they wished to forget things, but actually his family was quite similar to my own.

"Maybe you're surprised that we're going down to the Negev," Nimrod's father said. "It'll be hard for us, I know. But I want to be in a place where others haven't been yet. On a boat, you can sail for months before you see any sign of dry land. I hate the smooth deck and the waves that try to grab you. In the Negev, I can be the lookout on duty in the watchtower. Like on a pirate ship. The one who stands up above and sees the dry land before all the others do. Do you follow?"

"No! I don't follow you!" I stamped my foot. "You just moved into the neighborhood, and Nimrod has begun making friends. The Negev is a wasteland. Let others go there, why should you?"

Nimrod's father shrugged his shoulders. "Apparently we have more strength than they. There will be shade there, I promise you. We'll see to it. You'll be able to lie on your back and observe the heavens. He'll make new friends."

I wanted to express my worst fear, say that he might forget his former friends, but I didn't speak a word. Nimrod stood with his back to me. I yearned to go home.

"You'll visit us in the Negev. It's a small country. You can cross it in a day. People once crossed it by foot. Before we even arrived, other people were living here. Someday they'll live in peace with us. I hope that will happen in my lifetime. You'll come visit, won't you?"

He took me by the shoulder and turned me toward the iron bed. Now I saw the picture on the wall very clearly. It was a photograph of a very beautiful woman. Her blonde hair was plaited in a thick braid. She looked like the woman on the dish.

"Can you guess who she is?"

I nodded my head. "I'm familiar with pictures like that. She's dead, right?"

Nimrod's father shifted his face into the shadows. "We're all that's left," he said, "but still we managed to bring with us two important things." He bent over and pulled out a trunk from under the bed. It was the same trunk I had seen on the night they first arrived.

Nimrod said, "I'm not so sure, Dad. It's late. She has to go home now."

"But we haven't played in a long time. It's a special occasion. I already know that the young lady has good ears."

Then they played their instruments. Nimrod's father on the violin, and Nimrod on the recorder. I sat on the iron bed, and the gray woolen blanket scratched my legs. They sat on the opposite bed, pressed up against each other. Just one transparent thread tied me to them. Their music poured all around and hushed my anguished broken seed. Nimrod's fingers fluttered over the holes of his recorder. He played with his eyes shut. His hair had slipped down again and covered them, and he didn't have a free hand to readjust his hair.

I thought that maybe his mother in the picture could hear the notes. Maybe when they play she returns, because people in old photographs have ways of their own, exactly like blind people.

19

Grandpa said, "Last night, I heard some beautiful music. Your grandmother and I argued because of it. She said I was just imagining it."

I said, "You weren't, Grandpa. They really played instruments. Nimrod and his father."

And I asked myself whether she had pictured Grandpa to herself all the years of their separation—even after he'd sent her a divorce decree by mail. And if she'd cried.

Perhaps that was her final bout of tears, the most painful and most bitter. So, afterward, she had no more left. And then I thought that if she consented to take him back, she apparently never forgot him. Simha was right when she claimed a woman wouldn't forget her man. That I really understand. Like the mysterious girl who keeps sending Nimrod letters. I wish, though, that she would stop notifying him of her existence. . . .

The vacation shrank until there was just one day left. Tomorrow classes would begin. And Nimrod wouldn't be around anymore. Supposedly the van would show up in the afternoon and take them to the Negev. Hemda came upstairs this morning to ask me if I cared to join them on a last beach trip. "Everybody's going," she said.

"I don't think so."

"It'll be worth it. We'll be having all sorts of competitions there. Avigdor asked me to give you the message that he wanted you as part of his team."

"Thanks, but no."

"Did you know that our parents bought him a bike?"

"Really?"

"A Raleigh Sport with three gears. He won't let me touch it. He won't even agree to take me for a ride."

"I don't know how to ride a bike," I said. "I tried, and I fell each time."

Hemda hesitated for a second and then said, "He'd be glad to teach you."

The whole night the splinters inside me fluttered like tiny creatures. They learned how to speak, and now mocked me—he's going away, far, far from you. You won't see him. He'll forget you. And when I finally fell asleep, I dreamed that I was sailing on the Yarkon toward the sea, but not in a boat, on a huge seed instead. Sailing where the Yarkon merges with the sea—exactly at the spot where we released the fish—something white floats into view. "Stop!" I command the seed, and bend over into the water. The Yarkon of my dream was transformed into a wide river, wild and surging. A dangerous river, worthy of Mother's worries, not the calm line of water marking the

135

boundary of Tel Aviv. I pull as hard as I can on the white linen, but it is too heavy for me. "Nimrod!" I shout. "Come help me! At last I found Granny's wedding gown." I struggle and struggle, but somebody under the water keeps fighting me and pulling the material back into the water. "Wedding gowns are secret, and children mustn't see them. Or even dream about them." And I realize that it's the fish that we freed who is whispering to me from the water, and he is even laughing. Despite all that we had done for him, he remained loyal to Granny.

I woke up and found myself yanking on my blanket. It had fallen to the floor, and my fist was grabbing onto the hem of it. My hand was a stiff ball, and I was numb all the way to my shoulder.

I opened the window, and the sun gave me a warm embrace. It was the very sun that would send its flaming rays down on Nimrod's head in the Negev. It would face me and would face him, and only the sun would know. I couldn't be angry at it, for it had treated my flowerpot like a baby and made it sprout such an abundance of leaves. The awning covered the ring of soil now, and the foliage stood straight—well-protected. It was impossible to calculate the effort it made to grow.

I didn't go downstairs. I sat by the window and watched. Afterward, I knocked on Simha's door and asked her if I could step out on her terrace for a short while. Simha was delighted to have a visitor and took a dish full of taffy candies out of her cupboard and into the living room.

"This is to sweeten your first day of classes."

"Can I have two?"

Simha said, "Please," and added, "For the second day, also."

From her terrace, you could see the house that was closest to the Yarkon. I remembered the night they arrived. It was the same night that Grandpa and the green Plymouth came. I didn't know then that there would be any connection between those events.

Today of all days, when they were about to depart, their blinds were open. In Grandpa's room—one flight above—the shutter was closed. But for him, even when the shutter was raised to the top, it was always dark.

Simha asked, "What are you looking at?"

"I'm watching the workers."

"They're almost finished. Soon we'll have no more sand around here." Simha sighed. "We'll have more neighbors. My deceased used to say that as long as people keep coming, it's a sign that there's more room."

Nimrod stepped out onto his porch. The glaring light wrapped around him. He shook a white sheet, and then struggled to fold it by himself. Suddenly he sensed that I was observing him from the distance and he waved to me. I took one step backward.

Simha asked, "Isn't that the child who rides a bike?"

"He's not a child."

"Is he in your class?"

"No, he's leaving the street today."

"So, another child will take his place. The main thing is that your grandfather stays."

"I told you he wasn't a child."

"There's no need to grow up in such a hurry. Enjoy each

and every moment. When you're a child, you have no worries, right?"

Maybe she, too, had her doubts sometimes. Not everything that her deceased said was always true.

Before I made it back to my apartment, Nimrod was already there. "I came to say good-bye," he said. "And also . . . I wanted to see how the flowerpot was doing." He caressed the leaves. His touch was soft. They must have thought he was a butterfly and didn't object.

I said, "You treat it like a puppy."

"I once had a dog. When I was little. I used to tell it all my secrets. Funny, right? After all, a dog can't understand them."

"What secrets?"

"About my longings for my mother and father."

"Where were they?"

He didn't answer, he just concentrated on the leaves as if they were the most important thing in the world.

"You promised to take me to your nook along the Yarkon," he said.

I picked up the flowerpot in my arms and off we went. He wanted to hold it, but I wouldn't let him. He didn't mention the bike. He must have packed it already. But how could he ride a bike in a desert?

On the way, we passed Starkman's Grocery as Mother was arranging the milk bottles on the shelf. The chrome inspection tags glittered on them like jewelry.

"Your flowerpot needs a walk?" she laughed, which surprised me. I wasn't used to seeing her so happy.

Starkman said in Yiddish, "*Meshuganeh* kids." But he

really didn't mean crazy, and he gave us each a free stick of gum.

The bulrushes were very tall now. We blazed a trail, like in a jungle, until we found the small clearing. We sat on the dry ground, and I placed the pot between us. Nimrod took out a penknife from his pocket and cut down a bulrush.

We were silent.

His blond head was bowed, and he made a hole in the reed.

"We're missing a cello."

"What?" I asked.

"My mother. She played cello. She was a much more talented musician than my father or me. I could barely blow the recorder, since I was so young."

He placed his lips on the bulrush, but only a faint puff came out. I wanted to try, too, but I didn't dare ask.

Nimrod stripped the reed clean and made some more holes.

"It has to work. These were the original recorders. In Greek mythology, they tell about a certain god named Pan. Ever hear of him?"

I shook my head from side to side.

"He had horns on his head and the hooves of a goat instead of feet. He was very ugly and very miserable. He thought nobody loved him. He would hide in the bushes and make all kinds of noises."

"Why did he hide?"

"Maybe he was running away from somebody. Maybe

they were chasing him and persecuting him. Maybe they thought he was a Jew."

Nimrod brought the bulrush close to his lips. This time a faint but shrill sound emerged.

"You see?"

"But it makes no sense," I said. "When you hide, you must be extra careful not to make any noises."

"Or use them as camouflage. I know all of the Christian prayers. If you woke me up in the middle of the night, I'd immediately say, 'Ave Maria, oh Holy Mother.' "

"Is that a prayer for your mother?"

Nimrod put the bulrush against his lips and blew as hard as he could.

"My father placed me in a monastery after mother died. They promised to take good care of me until the war ended. There was a nun there called Aunt Teresa who watched over me. I loved her, and now she sends me letters. My father worked in the Gdansk shipyards disguised as a Pole. Even though Pan was ugly, he was merry, too. Do you know the legend about the bulrushes?"

"I didn't know anybody wrote legends about them." I grabbed a bulrush nearby and saw how firmly attached it was to the ground. I was barely able to move it.

"Bulrushes guard the notes inside them. They protect them as if they were their children. It isn't the wind that plays them. People are wrong. It's very simple. When they sense that two people are in love, they suddenly pipe up together in unison."

"Those letters . . ." I said. "I told the mailman that there was nobody with that name in our building."

Nimrod gripped the bulrush as hard as he could, his

wrists whitened and then his cheeks, too. "My name . . . isn't really Nimrod. I'm Janek Orlovski. Listen! The bulrushes are playing! Listen!"

I touched the reed he was holding, but he wouldn't let go of it. My finger covered one hole. "My name is Gershona. The kids call me Gershona Primadonna. You must know that already."

"Listen how they can make such wonderful music. They're just bulrushes growing on the banks of the Yarkon, and it's not even a river."

I didn't hear a thing. The shattered seed in me was shaking wildly and I couldn't pay attention.

"Janek," I said, "you're really Janek . . . "

He released the bulrush and let it fall into my open hand.

"I wanted a new name. I chose Nimrod myself. Know who he was? A hunter in days of old. The first one after the Flood. Even Aunt Teresa knew about him. She knew the Book of Genesis by heart. She knew the whole Bible. She called it the Old Testament, and wanted me to remember everything in it. So that when my father came to get me afterward, I wouldn't forget that I was Jewish. At night, when Aunt Teresa would put out the light, I was afraid that he wouldn't ever come back for me. The problem was that she couldn't accept my real name. For her, I'll always be Janek. Will you write to me while I'm in the Negev?"

"But I'll put Nimrod on the envelope."

"And I'll call you Gershona-Shona, the different Gershona. You think your name is ugly? But what's in a name?"

"I don't even know whose name it once was. He was some child that they won't tell me about."

"People don't tell secrets that hurt."

He took back the bulrush, and the touch of his fingers was like a caress. He placed it on the flowerpot, and the leaves didn't object. "It's yours now," he said.

"But I wouldn't ever be able to play it."

"You'll even be able to ride a bike. You'll see, Gershona-Shona. One day your little feet will push the pedals and you'll cruise and cruise. . . ."

A gust of wind suddenly shook the bulrush and the leaves. He embraced the flowerpot.

"Shall we pull them up?" he asked tenderly.

We carefully took out the radishes. From out of the brown soil emerged two purplish balls that had been in hiding all this time. They were perfectly ripe. We cleaned the radishes in our hands and on our shirts, and then ate them both. "One we'll set aside as a memento," said Nimrod and patted the single plant remaining. I chewed my radish, and the taste was tart. Tears jumped out of my eyes immediately. The sun hid behind the eucalyptuses, and we rose to leave. Nimrod ran his hand across the row of bulrushes.

"Who wrote that legend?" I asked.

He was quiet, and only when we reached my house and Grandpa's did he whisper, "I made it up."

20

No matter how hard I tried to lengthen the way home, I couldn't succeed. My heart hoped so much that, once at least, time would pass slowly, for my sake. But all the things we hadn't managed to tell each other now galloped through my head in a wild stampede. I thought in despair, When will we ever have time enough?

The van was already parked outside the house. Gray, horrendous, completely covered in tarpaulin. The vehicle lay in silent ambush, like a thief. Nimrod became tense and quickened his stride. The journey became even shorter. I felt I was running after him now. His father's head burst from the window. "What's the matter with you?" he shouted. "We're ready to leave any minute. I already loaded almost everything. All that's left is your trunk."

When he looked at me, the anger on his face vanished, and he smiled.

"Just one more minute, I want to say good-bye to Grandpa." Nimrod made his request, and his father continued smiling at me as though he hadn't heard a thing.

"Your grandpa did a smart thing by coming back to Israel. He had no other place to go, you understand? And there are doctors galore, perhaps even better ones than in America. . . ."

"I don't think Grandpa will ever see again," I said.

"A girl your age shouldn't always see the black side of things. When I load a ship and the sweat crawls down my back, I always think about the moment when they'll be unloading the crates in some port at the other end of the sea. I long for the sea."

I asked, "And how do you know in advance whether the ship will ever arrive?" But Nimrod's father didn't wait to answer me. He raced upstairs. Maybe he never heard my question.

They sat by the radio. Grandpa had spent the whole summer that way, listening to broadcasts in foreign languages, all the while turning the knobs. He continued playing the "Bureau for Missing Relatives" program, from start to finish. One day I asked him who it was he hadn't located yet, but he gave me no response, he simply turned the knob to another station. Nimrod loved to play with the knobs, too, and he no longer even needed to ask permission.

Grandpa said, "Turn, turn. In the Negev, you won't have a radio."

We heard the static interrupt the music and cut it short without any consideration. Nimrod smiled, "That's what happens on father's ships, when they try to radio ashore. I'm going to miss the sea, too."

144

Granny entered, with a full tray in her hands. Her holiday glasses stood tall around a plate of cookies, and she announced that she had just now removed them from the oven. She was wearing one of her marvellous dresses again. Now I was convinced that her wedding dress must have been unique. Too bad I missed out on it.

"We heard you playing the other night. It's a pity . . . now all I have is the radio," said Grandpa.

I toyed with the reed recorder, which was in my blouse pocket, and I set the flowerpot securely on my lap. The last plant didn't look lonesome, on the contrary—it waved its leaves jauntily. Grandpa smiled at me. "You go around with all your treasures, child?" Even if he called me Gershona, it wouldn't bother me. What is a name, after all? Just a costume that one gets used to.

Grandpa requested that Nimrod play a final small concert for him.

"But the violin is missing. And the cello hasn't been around for a long while."

"Never mind," said Grandpa, "the recorder is good enough. I'll fill in the rest myself . . . in my head."

Granny remained standing. Always on the threshold—not in the room itself, but also not in the corridor. Grandpa and I sat on the sofa and were a real audience. Nimrod ran to fetch his recorder from the empty apartment. Grandpa's hand rested on my shoulder as he played. I thought of people whose touch is like that of a butterfly. The high-pitched notes sailed through all the rooms, touching the walls and bouncing back. I wasn't able to decide if it was a sad melody or if it only sounded that way in my ears. As he came to the final section of the piece, we heard the motor of the van revving up. It roared like a hungry lion that had no patience left in him.

Grandpa suggested that I stand on the porch to watch them driving off, but I refused. I shut my eyes as tightly as I could, until I felt every muscle in my forehead and temples contract. Since then, I always shut my eyes when someone says good-bye to me. We stood in the room, and Grandpa held my hand. For a moment I was with him, the blind man, in total darkness.

To me, he will always be Nimrod the hunter of old, even if he keeps getting letters with foreign stamps on them. In the end, Aunt Teresa herself will have to accept that she can no longer call him Janek. Janek isn't the name fit for the Negev. Not that Gershona is a name fit for Tel Aviv, or anywhere else for that matter.

Outdoors, the racket went on and on. Grandpa sat with his back to me and listened to the news in English. He didn't ask me to read him the New York Stock Exchange, and I didn't insist on it, either. It was difficult for me, though, to sit in one place, so I went looking for the newspaper anyway. And Grandpa said, "It's not important. I'm not there, after all." He said it as though he had made peace with the fact that he would never again see the city with the tall towers. Although, of course, he could always—in his corridor—climb to the top story of the Empire State Building.

Again, that uproar of whistles and hoots, stubbornly repeating themselves. My heart missed a beat. For a second, I thought they had changed their minds, that the van was back. It wasn't so simple to exchange the sea for a desert. Or to go from Janek to Nimrod. But it was just my father

146

pressing against the horn of the green Plymouth, without letup. I didn't want to get up. My legs felt like two heavy stones. I waited until the shrill blast had stopped, but in its stead came a loud rapping on the door. My father wasn't a quitter.

Grandpa said, "Open up for your father. He hasn't a drop of patience." And there was no anger in his voice. Granny hugged Daddy. She always acted as though he had just returned from some distant spot or was about to leave any minute for a thousand-year voyage.

"You went out for a stroll?" asked Daddy.

"We were in a far-off place," said Grandpa, and turned off the radio.

Daddy was confused. He looked at me.

"Yes," I said, "we were in a far-off place, but we came back."

I approached the radio, wanting to jump inside it, become a long whistle that could silence the music.

"I can't find today's newspaper," apologized Daddy.

"It's not important. I already heard everything on the radio. They say it'll rain tomorrow. That's strange, isn't it? After all, we're in the middle of summer."

"It's already the tail end of summer," said Daddy, "and in this country, you can always expect surprises."

"Surprises don't come from countries, they come from people."

Daddy looked as if he'd been scolded. I said in my heart that he was not just my father but Grandpa's son, even though it was altogether hard for me to think of him as somebody else's child.

I was still in shock. I didn't utter a word until we got downstairs.

"I don't need a ride," I said. "I can walk home. It's not dark yet." But Daddy asked me to get in the car. I sat next to him and didn't look back at the last house at the end of the block. The Plymouth glided up the road, and Daddy went right past our house. "This is it," he said, "the final ride. Enjoy every minute of it. I sold the car."

"You sold it? Why?"

Daddy drove with one hand, and with the other, he vaguely sketched something in the air.

"What do I need a car for? To drive Mother to Starkman's Grocery? The Plymouth doesn't suit this street. She doesn't belong; she's a car without any friends."

"Really?"

"Also, I still can't park it right. It's too big a car. Mother's right. The car just doesn't fit in here. I feel awkward when everybody stares at me. Know what they think? That we're filthy rich."

"And what are we really?"

"Just ordinary people. Father, mother, daughter, grandmother—and now a grandfather, too. A family."

He pointed the Plymouth on the road to Haifa. The Yarkon was at our backs. "You're driving back to the port, Daddy?" I asked, and in my head flickered the picture, as in a magic lantern, of Daddy standing on that boat with the sign hanging from his neck, declaring his name.

His glance was penetrating. He was looking at me, not at the road, as if I were somebody different now—I was afraid we'd have an accident.

"You see a lot of things that you don't talk about."

I didn't answer. My hands trembled a bit and I stuck them onto the flowerpot, which rolled with every swerve of the Plymouth.

"I'd like to tell you something now. It's your present for the new school year. Mother and I . . . in a few months you're going to have a brother or sister."

The pot slipped from my hands and fell to the floor of the car.

"Mother's pregnant?" I sprang from the seat and my head smacked the roof. "Really? I won't be an only child anymore?"

Daddy gripped the wheel with both hands. A smile flooded his face. "Not so fast. We'll all have to wait patiently. And by next summer, we'll be quite a big family. We'll have to take a picture standing in a row."

"In the closet . . ." I said, "there's an old brown photograph of a boy. . . ."

Daddy simply said, "Gershon was Mother's younger brother."

We drove on. Daddy turned on the headlights, even though the sky was still keeping a close eye on the red color of the sun. It didn't want to part company that quickly. I felt that Gershon was there now with Nimrod's mother, and I also felt that the sky didn't need to be so grieved over the loss of the sun, because they would see each other tomorrow.

"The flowerpot broke, Daddy," I said. "I'm very sorry. I got the car dirty."

"It's nothing. We can clean it up. We'll scrub her and polish her, so the next owner will get practically a new car. He won't notice anything wrong. Too bad for the pot, though. But you finally got something to grow there?"

I ran my fingers through the scattered clods of earth on the floor, and found the last radish—a very small ball, which my fist covered completely. The violet hue absorbed the final rays of the sun now.

"That radish didn't get a chance to grow fully," said Daddy, "but I'm willing to taste it."

I cleaned it off on my blouse, exactly the way I had done it with Nimrod. Daddy bit into it and drove, bit again and drove, until the radish was gone.

"It has the taste of the earth in it, but it's still yummy," he said. Only then did I notice that we were back in town. We drove along the Yarkon on the way home. The dusk deepened. What a shame, I thought—now that Daddy had finally mastered the Plymouth, he was selling her.

There was a sudden chill in the air. I no longer asked why they hadn't invited me to the wedding, or how Granny could love Grandpa after thirty-five years of separation, or why he had returned to her all of a sudden. I was through with asking those questions.

By the building entrance, Avigdor was riding a home-made scooter, not a Raleigh Sport with three gears. When he saw us, he yelled: "Gershona, Gershona, we're starting a new garden tomorrow!"

As we stood near the steps, just before we began climbing, I heard them. As if an entire orchestra had burst into music. They were playing and singing in unison. I couldn't tell whether it was instruments or voices, all I knew was that they had to be the rushes—those reeds along the Yarkon River.

ABOUT THIS BOOK

Many stories begin with "Once upon a time," but Tel Aviv is very much a real place—a city of white houses built on white sands, on the coast of the Mediterranean. "Once" in this book is the year 1958. Tel Aviv was expanding then, with new neighborhoods everywhere. The houses, with many balconies and windows, were small and close together.

Israel is not rich in water, so the Yarkon River, to the north of the city, is considered a great body of water. In fact, it is a creek! But for the children of Tel Aviv it was, and still is, a real river, a place to escape to, a haven of nature and imagination. On the banks of the Yarkon, eucalyptuses and bulrushes grow, and children make kites and boats from their stems.

In 1958, Israel celebrated her tenth birthday. Gershona is two years older; her father tells her that she should feel responsible for Israel, as she would for a younger sister. Since her birth, Israel has had to face much hardship and many wars. Two years before this story takes place, the Sinai War broke out, a war that Gershona remembers well because her mother stored food in fear of a possible siege.

The 1950s were not easy years for Israel's inhabitants. New immigrants poured into the country from the four corners of the world. These were different people, from places at great distances from one another, and they were unified only by their Jewish identity and Jewish fate. Many of them altered the old traditions to some extent. After six working days, the Sabbath (Saturday, a day of rest and prayer for religious Jews) became a day to enjoy with family and friends and for relaxing on a nearby beach.

These were years of modest material existence. Food supplies and clothes were rationed. Cars were rare, ice was brought from a factory because there were no refrigerators, and people cooked on kerosene burners instead of stoves. Telephones seemed magical; they could be found in only one place in each neighborhood, usually the grocery store. Life was quite exciting and promising, though, because this small piece of land was for so many people their first true *home*.

Many of the people who came to Israel were scarred by the Holocaust. Gershona's mother survived several years in a concentration camp. Sometimes people who thought their loved ones were lost found a surviving relative, but for many the loss and sorrow were permanent. Families used to listen to a daily broadcast on the radio, "The Bureau for Missing Relatives," still hoping to hear a message from their lost ones. However, one challenge united them all—building a new life and opening a new page in Jewish history.

In a way, both Gershona and Israel are growing side by side, struggling to become . . . themselves.